Advance praise for *The Spanish Teacher*

"*The Spanish Teacher* is fecund with nationalism and its protagonist's dream of liberation from the subtler forces of imperialism. The breakdown of this culture can be witnessed not merely among the people, many of whom live in poverty, but more cruelly through the social progress which is promised to them—painted signs announcing new apartment buildings, a woman's clinic, children's nursery, sewer systems, supermarkets, and 'fountains to cool the afternoons.' But these improvements are not forthcoming as the politicians argue the benefits of one development over the other for their own gains. Ordóñez, a teacher at the American school in town, speaks out against these conditions to friends and in letters to the Minister of Education, activities which put his job at risk. Fearful that the brightest of his Spanish-speaking students may be siphoned off to America, he shouts, sings, stands on desks to convey the stories of heroes like Simón Bolívar, and especially to pass on the language of their culture. De la Cuesta's novel maintains an accumulating power which holds onto a reader's attention not only through the forceful figure of Ordóñez, but by demonstrating acutely how ordinary lives are impacted by the underlying social and political landscape. Compelling reading."

–Tom Tolnay, publisher, Birch Brook Press and author of *Selling America* and *This Is the Forest Primeval*

Advance praise for *The Spanish Teacher*

"Barbara de la Cuesta's *The Spanish Teacher* has everything to thrill you—pace, a great balance of description, gesture and action, charmed, perfectly-tuned dialogue, and most notably, a character we follow as closely and sympathetically as if we were living right there inside the story with him. Our fearless, keen, and wry protagonist occupies his native Venezuela with the power and grace of his beloved political heroes Simón Bolívar and Simón Rodríguez, teaching his students through song and antic story-telling, sitting daily in his town square writing thick personal and political journals, loving and devoting himself to friends, and eventually launching on a peculiar and surprising odyssey that hugely raises the tension of an already crisp, humming novel. While Ordóñez says to a friend, and us, that people will say of him 'He died in want.', we have the greatest time watching him live a total life, in dignity, in richness. So many books show us a character who seems to capably hang and move like marionettes from the strings of a fairly competent puppeteer, but rarely do we see a full drama like this, where every bit of the writing extends from, grows out of, is part and parcel with the author's complete realization of and connection to her character. From the first time we see Ordóñez on the terrace wrapped in his mule blanket watching the privileged Vice-Consul dressed as an Apache dancing with his wife, this book starts taking good, long, deep breaths, grows alive in us."

–Don Berger, judge for the Gival Press Novel Award

Other works by Barbara de la Cuesta

The Gold Rush (a novel)
If There Weren't So Many of Them (long poem)
Westerly (nonfiction)

The Spanish Teacher

by
Barbara de la Cuesta

Gival Press

Arlington, Virginia

Copyright © 2007 by Barbara de la Cuesta.

All rights reserved under International and Pan-American Copyright Conventions. Printed in the United States of America.

With the exception of brief quotations in the body of critical articles or reviews, no part of this book may be reproduced or transmitted in any form or by any means, graphic, electronic, or mechanical, including photocopying, recording, taping, or by any information storage or retrieval system, without the permission in writing from the publisher.

Published by Gival Press, an imprint of Gival Press, LLC.

For information please write:
Gival Press, LLC, P. O. Box 3812, Arlington, VA 22203.

Website: www.givalpress.com
Email: givalpress@yahoo.com

First edition ISBN 13: 978-1-928589-37-2
Library of Congress Control Number: 2007935324

Book cover artwork: "Mountain Scene and Broken Statue" by James Hartung.
Format and design by Ken Schellenberg.

WRAPPED in his mule blanket, Ordóñez stood in a corner of the terrace observing the Vice-Consul, Mr. Plimford, dancing with his wife. They were dressed as Apaches. Mrs. Plimford, whose name it was said was Dee Dee, had good legs and showed them off with sly sensuality

They had hired musicians, the best in the city, and the guitarist, Eusebio Vargas of the inward face, was just at that moment passing the beat of a *bolero* to the maraca player.

"What a man, this Eusebio!" someone cried and Ordóñez, looking upward at the fiery stars above the burning mountains, allowed himself to be stirred.

A pair, dressed to represent a Mexican wedding, danced the *bolero* in a studied way, but well. They wore masks, their hair tucked up but it was certain both were women. Ordóñez watched them, noting how the one smiled in ironic awareness of her pleasure, while the other moved in a trance of grave concentration that tugged at him until he moved across the terrace and interrupted them.

He spoke in English. "I would like to know who you are."

"But I can't tell you," said the one he had chosen, "It is Carnival."

This amused him. "I am here as myself, as Ordóñez," he said. "Ordóñez cannot afford a costume."

She knew him, from the *Colegio*.

"I think I have seen you before," he said.

"You have." Every morning, at ten, he stepped through the open air side of her classroom, to come to teach her children to sing *"La Cucaracha."*

He didn't begin dancing with her, merely stood with her hand in his. "But where, where did you come from?" He meant how had it been she, who had tugged at him thus...

• 1 •

"Warsaw," she said.

"Warsaw?"

"Warsaw, New York."

He was bewildered.

"They named it in a fit of distraction," she said. "It's a little place."

"We have little towns," he said, "Ah, they are named to great purpose, great purpose. Reform, they are called, or Purity! Ha! Ha! Like the cook's daughter who is called Purificación, the slut."

She laughed, looking into his face. He moved her to one side of the terrace. The Plimford's house, which had once been the Italian consulate, overlooked Miraflores. You could see the length of Roosevelt Avenue as far as the British school. "I have been to Philadelphia," he said. "Do you know Philadelphia?"

"I've never been there."

"I accompanied a priest to a congress at Villanova College. One should avoid traveling with priests. 'We are going to a country without a soul,' he told me. 'You must take care.'"

She moved back to find a seat on the low terrace wall. The musicians had finished a set and were smoking in a corner, their instruments resting on the wall. He followed her, noting the small, sleek head and slender shoulders. He had seen her before.

"We went on a 'C' liner called 'The City of Tunja.' There was a terrible storm. He came to my bunk. I thought he wanted to throw me overboard, like Jonah. Ha! But he only wanted to give me confession. I got away from him in Philadelphia."

"I'm glad of that."

Another mountain was burning, over above the Malaria

Station. "Why do they burn?" she asked.

"The farmers burn off the trees, so cattle can graze on the new grass when the rains come. They should not do it. It is on the radio every hour."

"*Hola!*" Ricaurte's voice issued from inside a *papier maché* mask. "Eusebio Vargas is unhappy with the punch."

"Is there rum?"

"Perhaps in the kitchen. The costumes are going to be judged and I don't want to miss it. Then I am to sing a ballad of Evaristo Gil's."

She knew Ricaurte. He was the other one, the other Spanish teacher to her little charges, sons and daughters of Firestone executives.

"I'll look for the rum," Ordóñez said. He turned to her. "You will come?" She nodded and followed him down the flight of stairs to the kitchen, where a hired waiter found a bottle of Ron Viejo. "That will do," said Ordóñez. "Eusebio Vargas must have something decent to drink." "Yes, yes," the waiter nodded. "There is no one like Eusebio Vargas."

They returned upstairs with the rum and found the musicians seated around a laundry tub out on the roof.

"Now this you could call something to drink," said the maraca player, passing the glasses around.

Ricaurte's performance could be heard through the open window. "It is a *copla* of Guillermo Lara's," said the guitarist.

"No, it is by Evaristo Gil," said Ordóñez.

"Ah, yes."

"River that reached out and took the girl / Daughter of the tavern keeper..."

"I had a friend, a taxi driver, who sang that," said the maraca player. "He could wring tears from the Horned One,

• 3 •

I swear."

"That is true," said Eusebio Vargas.

"White-skinned, she was, and well-formed..."

"That is poetry. That is poetry!" said the maraca player.

"For poetry you need rum," said Eusebio Vargas. "Our friend Ricaurte, I'll bet, drinks vermouth like the ladies, or gin."

The maraca player had brought out a box of firecrackers, which he began lighting from a cigarette, tossing them out over the terrace wall. He offered one to Ordóñez's companion. "Will the Señorita try...?"

"They are dangerous," Ordóñez told her. "If one is put together upside down, it explodes in one's face."

"I'll throw it quickly," she said. She held the little rocket over the wall, flipping it outward toward the center of the little park below. It shot sideways, and returned to sputter out at their feet.

"See, they do not hurt you," said the maraca player.

"A miracle," said Ordóñez. "A miracle we are not all killed every March. Four or five years ago, the row of shacks on Roosevelt Avenue where they sell the fireworks went up, one after another. Boom boom boom, a chain reaction like your atomic bomb," he said to her.

"It is not my atomic bomb," she said.

"Yes, it is. What's here is mine. What's there is yours."

The maraca player offered Ordóñez the last rocket. He took it and handed it to her. "Would you like to take another chance, *Señorita*, that the charge is correctly inserted in this little invention?"

"With pleasure," she said, lighting it and holding onto its stem until the last minute, before tossing it down into the street.

AT one o'clock, they left the Plimford's and followed the musicians to the Obelisk Grill.

"Eusebio Vargas must be forgiven a fondness for the verses of Guillermo Lara," said Ordóñez, as they walked toward the river.

"I don't understand," she said.

"They are ballads of taxi drivers, who listen all day on their car radios to *Romances de Hoy*. How nauseating! Evaristo Gil and his 'Infant white as the Child Jesus!' Holy Mother! Has no one ever looked at an infant in this country?" said Ordóñez. He stopped to drink from the bottle of *Ron Viejo* he had carried away from the Plimfords' kitchen. "Do you want?"

"No, thank you."

"It is we are a people who can intoxicate ourselves with words. Our national vice."

Del Rio Avenue followed the dry bed of the Humboldt River as far as the deep canyon where the Barrio Santa Ana spilled down the sides of the hills that held aloft the shacks of Terrón Colorado.

"Our nourishment flows out of us," he said. "I feel sometimes that I am dying of discussions. Do you understand? When El Cacique, our illustrious dictator, was in the twenty-second year of his reign, we plotted to kill him. We met in Roberto Pino's house and talked about it till morning. It lasted seventeen years, our discussion and, in the meantime, El Cacique took to his bed to die, of natural causes. I became ill. I would have died too, if I had not discovered a cure…"

"What was it?" she asked.

"I took a walk. Five hundred miles, from Malaganueva to Los Chorros. In the company of a mule. It was a mule capable of long silences. We exchanged, along the whole way, only two or three comments: how the sand on the banks of the Málaga River is gray, while the bed of the Culebra is white."

"And you recovered?" she asked, wondering how one could be attracted to a man with this suddenness, simply because he tells these absurd...

"Yes. That was many years ago. I was a journalist. It was in 1959," he said. "What were you doing in 1959?"

She thought he might be trying to calculate her age. "I suppose I was sitting on the floor piling blocks," she said.

"In Warsaw, New York?"

"Yes."

"What kind of a place is that?"

"I grew up on a farm, on a dairy."

"Ah, so..."

"Like one of those heroines of an animal saga," she laughed.

"What is that?"

"A kind of a story we have for children who have no pets."

"Ah, for everyone you have something. Why did you come here?"

"An ad in the *New York Times*," she said. "Teachers Abroad."

"And you wanted to come here, precisely here?"

"No...I think it was Spain."

"Ah, you ask for Spain and you get here. A pity."

"It hasn't mattered," she said.

He stopped her under a street lamp, took off her hat and mask. It was a neat, focused face, evenly freckled, with dark hair drawn back.

"It's what I've wanted," she said.

"What is that?"

"To walk out on the street in my costume."

"Ha! Like the maid servants they quit their jobs before Carnival and dance four nights till dawn in the Barrio Colorado. Then after, you will see them dragging their tin trunks up and down the streets of Alta Mira and Santa Rita looking for another job. So, you are a teacher."

"Yes. My name is Dorie West."

"I am a teacher too."

"I know."

The guitarist, Eusebio Vargas, had moved to fill in with a group in the Barrio Candelaria only the maraca player was at the grill when they arrived. Ordóñez invited him to share a plate of meat pies.

"Mr. Plimford does not keep a group long enough to count for a night's work," the maraca player said. "And then he lets you go too late to find another employment. It would be more profitable to play till three in the Casa del Pueblo, though they only give you ten pesos an hour. You wanted to hear Eusebio Vargas in another set?"

Ordóñez nodded.

"Wait a bit. Macario will be back, and we'll play you a *Merengue*."

They didn't wait, but walked up to Santa Ana Avenue and crossed the Calle Quinta Bridge into the Plaza La Callada. There was a large marble base without a statue. "What was it?" she asked.

"El Cacique," he said. Our Great Man. We are ashamed of him now, and we tumble his statues into the grass."

"You wanted to kill him once," she said.

"Nevertheless, he was our Great Man."

"A tyrant," she said. She had read a book. "He put innocent people in chains."

"My house is three blocks from here," he said. "Shall we go there?"

"Yes," she said. Her feet were aching. He led her past the darkened flank of the Chapel of San Judas, through another little plaza with its tired gestures of ragged palm and rudimentary fountain, and down the narrow Cuarta Bis Street to his door, which he opened with three separate keys. Inside, he told her to wait while he went to the kitchen to find a candle stuck in a saucer, which he lighted to avoid turning on the overhead bulb in the parlor.

"Sit here." He indicated one of two leatherette chairs. "Wait, I will wipe it." He took a rag from under a cushion.

"The street is unpaved and there is always dust..." He was quickly sober, appalled by the house as she must see it: cramped parlor with pictures his sister cut out of *Hogar* and taped crookedly to the walls, the hens roosting on the sills, the cock in a cage on top of the refrigerator. He excused himself to go back to the kitchen and find a bottle of rum from which he swigged twice before he returned to her, thinking, how could I have lived so long this way and never noticed...?

She waited, becoming sober. He seemed gone a long time. There were students' exercise books lying all over the floor. She picked one up and read:

Simón Bolívar, until he was six years old, ran naked as a savage. His tutor instituted a system of instruction based on Rousseau's Emile. *To this we owe our liberation from Spain...*"

Ordóñez returned, handed her a glass. "My wife is dead," he said to her.

"I am sorry...

"She was my first cousin. I always preferred the women of my family to others. She left me three children. My sister Alicia cares for them."

"What are their names?" she asked.

"Lily and Rita, the girls and Luis. He is ten. In an hour my sister will get up to go to Mass."

"Shall we go in there," she said, pointing to the door of a room off the patio.

"Do you want to?" he asked.

"Yes. I don't want…them, anyone to see us."

"I have a wish to embrace you…"

"I too."

"Have you had lovers?"

"One," she said.

"Come," he said, and led her into the dark room, where he stretched wearily on the bed, "Come, lie here beside me and tell me, who was your lover?"

"He was a boy I knew after college, a motion study consultant."

"And was he a good lover, this motion study consultant?"

"I used to imagine there might be better," she said.

"And what happened to him?"

"He went to California," she said.

"Ah…" These details interested him. He hadn't bothered to know a North American woman since Mrs. Hicks of The Society of Practical Yoga, whom he had known in Philadelphia. She used to ask him to lie on her rug and concentrate on the Totality of his Being on the ceiling. It had been by way of forgetting the priests in his life. From her he had learned how North American women combined wantonness with a fretful morality.

"Could you take off your shoes? Ah, that's a good girl. You would think," he said, turning to her and putting a hand on her breast, "You would think that such a man as Ordóñez could not please a woman. But the truth is he has always done so. Can you believe that?"

"Yes, "she said soberly.

"Ah, Warsaw, I have slept in this miserable house, in this miserable bed for seventeen years. I will die here, no doubt." He lay back on the pillow. "They will say of me as they said of Cervantes, 'He died in want.'"

She laughed at him. "Can you open your blouse for me?" he asked. Her costume was formidably buttoned. She obeyed. He watched her, thinking: So, right off, she has settled the matter of whether I must go to the trouble of seducing her. It touched him, this educated woman hastening like a kitchen maid to confess a past. He got up to take off his shirt and pants. "There is a story told of El Cacique," he said. "He used to wear a broad Panama hat with his uniform, instead of a visor cap and one of his lieutenants said to him once, 'My dear General, it is the hat that brings your luck on the battlefield.' 'Ah, no, my man,' said El Cacique. 'It is I, I, who bring luck to the hat...'"

He tossed his shirt and pants into a corner and lay down again. "And what will they say of Ordóñez? 'He died in want,' they will say. *'Pobre de* Ordóñez, he died in want.'

"He always knew, El Cacique, if someone was plotting to kill him. They called him *El Brujo,* the Wizard," he said.

"Is that why you couldn't kill him?"

"El Cacique put a thousand innocent people to chains, and Ordóñez cannot even raise his voice to Chula the washerwoman, who deserves it. No, it was all talk. We were journalists, dreamers. We thought we would save this wretched..."

There came a sudden sound over their heads, like a slipping of tiles. She sat up. "What was that?"

"It is the roosters. The street lamp shines in the window and they think it is the dawn."

"No, no...someone running, on the roof"

"Paco, did you hear his sister's voice in the patio? There is a thief!"

"Damn!" He pulled his pants on again.

"They were in the Villamarin's kitchen and took the Osterizer!" the sister cried. She was pounding on the door.

"Where are they now?" he shouted.

"On the roof! They are on the roof!" shouts from the street could be heard. There was a pounding on the front door. "He is on your roof, Ordóñez! He must come down in your patio. You must let us in!"

"No, no! from the street. He will cross over by way of the Villamarins'! The damned watchman is never where he can be of use. He is always smoking in the widow by Berrios's doorway!"

"Ay, but the wretches have been at the Ochoas also! They took a watch off the night table and Don Roque's pants off the chair!"

The watchman arrived, blowing a whistle. Dorie went to the window, saw a figure drop from the roof above the bedroom into the street, where he was grabbed by the watchman and a man who had come out of the house nearby.

"Ah, there, for once he has served his purpose," called the woman across the way. "There, there! They have caught him. What is he? Young or old?"

"Young," called the watchman.

"Shame! A shame to his mother!"

"And the Osterizer and Don Roque's pants?"

• 11 •

"He must have dropped them over the back wall of the Hurtados'. When Don Rafa went around there, they ran this way!" "Look, here! He has taken the pants to one suit and the coat to another! Poor fool. If he'd gotten away, he wouldn't have had a suit, or Don Roque either!"

"The police, Madame, have the police been called?" demanded the watchman.

"Yes, yes, Alfredo has gone to Lino's to call. The second time this week. What shall we do for a night of peace? Do you have a firm hold on him, my man?"

"I do," said the watchman. "I have him here by the wrists and by the ankle...One lifts the ankle thus, and the subject cannot..." He lifted the leg higher in the air, and the boy, who had been balancing on one foot, suddenly wrenched free and fled down the street.

Ordóñez, who had just gotten his pants on, stumbled to the window to witness the flight.

"Oh, the wretches!" He sat down on the bed with his head in his hands. "What have we got here? What have we got here? A thief who cannot steal properly, and a watchman who cannot watch properly! Oh God! What can one expect in such a country!" He lay back on the bed and pulled the covers over himself.

It was nearly dawn.

"My dear Warsaw, you must forgive me," he mumbled. "You must forgive me...this ridiculous event...I find myself incapacitated by this ridiculous event..."

She began to laugh. He was grateful for her laughter. He might become very fond of this woman who had gravely watched him open her blouse buttons and who was now laughing as if that unbuttoning had never taken place. She sat at the foot of the bed and bent over his knees, as the paroxysms caught her up.

It didn't matter, did it? she thought. She would see him. He would come through the coleus border to teach her children *"La Cucaracha…"*

He fell asleep moaning, "Oh the wretches." She slept also, curled up at the bottom of the bed. An hour later, while the sister was out at Mass, she found her way out and took a taxi from the Calle Quinta bridge.

ORDÓÑEZ rose at noon, forgetful of the girl and of the thief in the night. At three, he went out to buy the lottery at Barroso's. Alicia gave him fifty pesos every week to buy her a fraction of the ticket. He had a cup of chocolate and a hard-boiled egg at the Turko's, and then took up his accustomed place on a bench in the Plaza Libertador and opened his notebooks to await the arrival of Don Tiburcio Gómez at the Café of The Thousand and One Nights.

But Don Tiburcio didn't arrive. He hadn't come to the café for three days now. Was he suspicious? "You're a deep one with your notebooks, Paco," Tiburcio said. "God knows what you're up to." Does he flatter himself with being the object of my research? Ordóñez wondered. Is he frightened? It wasn't like him. Tiburcio was one to scoff. The schoolteacher with his notebooks—how futile…

Still, it was an employment with a noble history. Balzac had followed his countrymen around with a notebook…or had it been Gorki?

His head ached. It was a riot and a good day for research. He had drunk too much. He recalled, now, the girl—her grave, steady look. "I have not had many lovers, but I have had one…"

Ha! She was a teacher…he had seen her…

• 13 •

Oh, but he had drunk too much, and there had been a thief. And he had not behaved well.

The palms stirred dry as a bone overhead. A sultry wind blew up dust in the plaza. The mountains were burning—one slope above La Victoria, another to the west of Las Tres Cruces. It was hot. It would be fine thing, he thought, if the plaza had fountains...

"Ho!" Ricaurte stood above him.

"Hello, my friend." Ordóñez rose. "Sit down, please. It's good to see you. I was just sitting here thinking how the designers of these little plazas we have in every town always seek some how shall I say it? Some ideal. They do not always succeed, as in Canterrana where they used dwarf palms, which are plebian palms, give no shade, and drop their leaves constantly, always creating garbage. Here, though, in this plaza, they have almost succeeded. But there should be fountains..."

"You are a fool, Paco," said Ricaurte.

"...and the fact that they have been repairing that section of Miranda Street for nineteen months now," he went on, "And that there is always dust...When Alfredo Cruz was mayor, they wanted to widen the street and put a row of fountains in the middle, did you know?"

"I don't concern myself about such things," said Ricaurte.

"Fountains would cool the afternoons, keep down the dust. The Lucianistas claimed there were no sewers in the Barrio Terrón, that the money should be spent on sewers and not Fountains. Cruz was thrown out because he made a speech supporting the Pisanista Party and so now there are no fountains and no sewers either."

"You are a fool, Paco," Ricaurte repeated bleakly.

Ordóñez laughed.

"So, you will be happy then, my man, teaching sixty sons of laundresses—dirty little *sambos* with 'their hands on their— you-know-what's under the desk...'"

"I don't know what you're speaking of."

"You are going to lose your job. You are going to lose your job at the *Americanos'* school. Have you not thought of it?"

"Of course." Ordóñez answered, "One thinks of it..."

"Then why do you continue to write letters to the Ministry of Education...?"

"Ah, man..."

"Signing 'Alcibiades.' Don't think I don't know about it. 'Alcibiades!' Tell me now, how many have you written?"

"Ricaurte, dear friend, I don't even know. It's an interesting thing. You write a letter and drop it in the letterbox. And the moment, the moment you release it from your hand, it no longer has any connection to you. It is in the hands of the Postal Service. It is like swallowing the host when you are seven years old—a release and you feel light; a larger agency has you in its hands. Listen, I have written a circular. I will go to the people. I will go to the people. I will make them feel ashamed."

"Ah, man, a circular and you are finished."

"You read it. I will show it to you. It is a reasonable proposal. Half of the day. Half of the day, the children shall study their native language. It is a reasonable proposal. I am a reasonable man."

"But why cannot you simply allow the *Americanos* to have their school as they wish? It is supposed to be for their children."

"But our children go to it."

• 15 •

"But they don't have to. They could go to our own..." Ricaurte took out a cigarette, lit it, and threw it away.

"Nonetheless, they *do* go. And they speak all day in a foreign language and know nothing of their own...so that they cannot even compose a sentence in their native language... they cannot even compose a letter of protest to their own minister of education, even if they should wish to...Even if they should wish to, Ricaurte!"

"Ah, Ordóñez..."

"And then they go off to West Point or to M. I. T. , and we are thus deprived of our ruling class, our scientists."

"So, what do you want, a law?"

"Of course, a law."

"We already have too many laws," Ricaurte said, exasperated. "Listen, I will not discuss it with you. Think of your children. You have lost one position; you will lose another. You will lose, also, your right to use the Postal Service. To Roberto Pino they did this. From him they took away the right to circulate his magazine. Any word that Roberto Pino writes cannot cross a state line. Is this what you are after? Think, Ordóñez, think, I beg of you..."

"Roberto Pino is known at this moment as 'Hippias Major.' His newspaper is transported by air; a company that makes corn chips carries it on their runs to make up the weight. They have a private plane rented from Aereolineas Sur."

"Yes, yes, a plane full of flatulence. Don't speak to me about Roberto Pino," said Ricaurte.

Ordóñez looked off across the plaza. "Don Tiburcio is not coming to the cafe today," he said to Ricaurte in Spanish— usually they conversed in English—"Perhaps Doña Reina has suffered gastritis again... What is it you say, *hombre*, about

Roberto Pino?"

"That they will catch him in the end, and you too," Ricaurte murmured frowning.

"I must do what I must," Ordóñez said

"Oh, well..." Ricaurte shrugged, lit another cigarette. "I saw you with the little American girl last night," he said.

"Who is that?"

"Miss West."

"Who?"

"Miss West who teaches at the *colegio* from which you will so imprudently have yourself dismissed."

"Ah, ha!" Ordóñez clapped his hand on his forehead. "I knew I had seen her before...I could not think!"

"I think that she likes you. I think that if I were you, Paco, that I would propose some...arrangement to her."

"You have no soul, Ricaurte."

"I know nothing of these matters. But I have never heard of such an extended grief, Ordóñez, even in a woman. Your wife is dead; she's been dead three years. You need a woman."

"If she were Lilia's type..." Ordóñez gathered his brows. "Ah, Ricaurte, now and then I see a woman with the Lilia's body on the street, at the butcher's buying an ox tail...and I think...it is against all reason, Ricaurte...I think that if I could take that woman who is buying an ox tail for soup straight home to my bed, neither of us speaking a word, then my pain could be soothed..."

"I know nothing of such things," said Ricaurte.

Ordóñez stared at him. If I could crawl inside Ricaurte, if I could reach that source of Ricaurte's ignorance then, also, I could be soothed...

Ricaurte stood up. "I must go. May I remind you again

you are a fool, in the matter of these letters…"

Ordóñez embraced him. "Goodbye, man. I appreciate that you think of me."

A fool, also, in the matter of Miss West, thought Ricaurte. As well as in the matter of Tiburcio Gómez, for your children are second cousins and might have something from him if you knew how to manage it."

So as not to have wasted the afternoon, Ordóñez noted Ricaurte's appearance in the notebook: *Ricaurte calls me a fool in the matter of the letters to the Minister of Education. I will lose my position at the Americanos' school, he says. It is quite possible. Yet I must do what I must do.*

The elevator boy with the pockmarked face greeted her.

"A pleasure, Madam…"

"A pleasure to see you, too," Dorie said. He took her down the two floors to the lobby. "Do you think it will rain?" she asked, keeping to their ritual. She had arrived during August storms, and took to asking the question before she went out. "In three hours," or "In forty-five minutes," he would answer sagely.

Now he answered, "No rain. The mountains are burning."

"Yes, I see," she said. "I wonder how the fires start."

"They start by themselves'," he said. "Heat of the sun."

"Could such a thing be so?"

She thought of Ordóñez. He would tell her the exact truth about some of these matters. Would he speak to her again? He had behaved badly, she supposed, at least in his own way of thinking. And so he was probably ashamed. Sad, she thought. Perhaps our friendship is over, not because of my expectation of him, but because of his own expectation of himself. Sad, she thought, sad and unnecessary.

The dining room was open. She decided to have breakfast. The waiter, like the elevator boy, spoke to her in simple sentences. "It does not rain now," he said. "The mountains are burning."

"Is it true," she asked, "that the sun sets the fires?"

"Not true," he said. "People set the fires. They burn the trees so that their cattle can graze on the new shoots."

"The elevator boy says the sun sets them," she said.

"Ah, the elevator boy is an ignorant person. He will tell you the first thing that comes into his head."

"He's a nice boy, still…"

"A nice boy, but ignorant. He has bad habits. You ask me why the mountain bums—if I do not know, I will tell you. I will say, I do not know."

"That's always best."

"Always best. You are right. The elevator boy is ignorant." The waiter said and left her.

You are letting him addle your brains, she told herself.

An underling waiter brought the tarry coffee and the boiled milk, along with a plate of corn pancakes left from supper. The hotel was failing. El Cacique had it built for his generals' pleasure; now the generals were back in Charagua and the hotel was half-empty. She looked at the two saucers under her cup, one smaller, one slightly larger. There was something bureaucratic about the repetition, and the two waiters for the simple order.

Beyond the lawns, with their faded red and white signs—
ON THIS SITE WILL BE CONSTRUCTED AN OLYMPIC

SIZE SWIMMING POOL—the mountains burned in two places. A fine soot drifted into the dining room, smudging the white tablecloth. General Le Funa moved across a patch of lawn on his white horse. Under an awning in front of the military stables, a group of waiters decorated a float for the Queen of the Sugarcane. She pulled the skin off the boiled milk—*la nata,* the waiter called it—filled the cup with the milk and tinted it with dark coffee.

Feli wasn't down yet. Dorie finished the coffee and went into the kitchen to get her lunch bag. "Is there white cheese?" she asked the *maitre*. He smiled at her. She was known in the kitchen as "The Señorita Who Thought the Plantain was a Banana." He cut her a slice from the large sweating cake of cheese on the counter, and wrapped it in wax paper for her.

Still no Feli.

She went out, sated with the simplicities of her hotel friendships, and crossed the lawn to the broad empty lots of Ciudad Jardín. More red and white signs here: ON THIS SITE WILL BE ERECTED THE CHILDREN'S PARADISE NURSERY... HERE WILL BE A MODERN SUPERMARKET... OUR LADY CLINIC WILL CONSTRUCT A NEW FACILITY... APARTMENT BUILDING OF SIX STORIES...

The hotel, standing up in bright white isolation, was the only building ever built.

At the kiosk, she had a second, better cup of coffee. The sun, a dusky orange, rested on the shoulder of the smoking mountain range. The bus turned the corner of Roosevelt Boulevard, two blocks below her, and at the same moment Feli emerged from the hotel. She would not make it.

"Would you wait a minute?" Dorie asked Franco the driver as she climbed on the bus.

"I'm late already," he said.

But Feli came, not even running, and fell beside her in the front seat.

They picked up two children in the Alta Mira sector, then plunged off Roosevelt Boulevard onto the ruinous road past the bullring and the State Hospital. The sun, moving up in the white sky, spread dusty light across the plain and across the lap of Father Jairo in the seat opposite. The priest, who taught a catechism class before school hours, took a lozenge from his lunch bag and sucked it noisily. He offered the bag across the aisle.

"Clears the sinus passages. Mint?" he said.

They accepted, and sucked on the candy.

"There is another fire." He pointed it out, behind the hospital, creeping downward toward the Barrio Terrón. "Last year they had to send the engineers. The military stables were threatened."

The Bournholm's maid came out of the house they rented on the Baptist Mission. Dick was sick and the children, too. The Bournholms suffered from dysentery.

Out of town now, they sped along the straight highway which ran the length of the broad valley. It was grassland, with gentle hummocks were green, in spite of the season, because of underground springs, coming ceaselessly to the surface, like the playground rocks at school.

The school was a mile and a half off the highway, on a dirt road winding up the slopes of Catalagrande. Feli's pale face looked bruised this morning; she endured the bucks and plunges of the bus. The barrack at San Isidro looked benign in the early morning quiet, its patios aflame with bougainvillea, and next to it was the state asylum where Dorie had heard they used to put Feli's friend Pepe Ochoa every month or two, when he went crazy drinking *Ron Viejo.*

Feli had lived three years with Pepe in two rooms in Barrio Colorado. A year ago he had gone on a cultural mission to Hungary and had never returned. "Why didn't you go home?" Dorie had once asked.

"Home?" Feli had said, looking vague. Born in Egypt of an Arab father and a Swiss mother, Feli, on the night of her first marriage to a Jew, was sent to prison with her husband and deported the next day on separate ships. They had met later, in Buenos Aires, but had quarreled and gone their own ways.

The school was set in a cow pasture, with low cement block buildings with Formica and glass panels, a disappointment to her when Dorie first set eyes on it; it didn't much matter now, for behind it were the mountains, visible because the classrooms all had an open side facing west. She had known mountains, New York State mountains but these could be hidden by the roof of a barn, or the branches of an oak. Not these. Today, in haze, they were a gray curtain below the white sky. The bus was late, so she crossed the grass, and entered her open-air class through the coleus bordering its side. *He* came in this way always, though it was urged on them to stay off the grass.

A notice sheet was left on her desk: Ditto machine is to be left on off-ink position. Another teacher, Miss Vitale, out with hepatitis. Sr. Ricaurte would substitute. His Spanish classes cancelled.

Enrique Fensterberg came in through the coleus border.

"I thought you were in religion class," she said.

"I thought you might need some help."

He was the most oppressively helpful boy in her experience. He could see she was simply staring out at the mountains.

"You corrected the science tests?" he asked.

"Not till Wednesday."

"I could read you off the answers while you checked. I did that for Miss Kearny."

"Who is that?"

"The second grade teacher. Three years ago. You wouldn't have known her. I'm the boy who's been in this school longest. We had our class in a kiosk with a thatch roof, and the rain came in..."

"I would have liked that," she said. "The kiosk, that is."

Enrique Fensterberg. The name represented one of odd South American unions like the Hotel Conahotu-Westerhotel or the companies: Hilares-Elephant, Avena-Quaker, Quimco-Celanese. Enrique's mother was Elena Rivas, daughter of a retired colonel who was related to the Zuloaga family that ran the cement plant. Father was Fensterberg of the Air Force Mission. On the whole a better marriage than Conahotu-Westerhotel, she thought, resulting in Constanza, Paca, Huberto, and Enrique, bright-eyed, ingratiating, glib in two languages.

The Protestant bus arrived. She lined the children up to go out and pick up rocks from the soccer field before the day became too hot. These were all wealthy children, but the principal, Mr. Hilyer, had Puritan principals he wished to instill.

They were playful, handing her quartz and fools gold to admire, and trading rocks among themselves. "It's a working time, no games," she reminded them, putting the beautiful rocks firmly in the burlap sack with the plain ones. Mr. Ricaurte stood on the edge of the field, surrounded by Miss Vitale's children. He held two small stones away from his tidy person with splayed fingers.

"What causes this fresh crop every week?" she asked.

"It is a phenomenon of this region," he said. "The wretches of Chibchas in the mountains have been piling rocks for centuries, to pen their beasts, mark their land..."

"I saw, yes and there are mounds..." She had taken a bus to Mercaderos a week before Christmas.

"The mounds mark graves, some say," Ricaurte told her. "They are very old; no one knows how old. Three thousand years perhaps."

She went back to call the children, picking up two large stones as she walked and carried them to the pile near the drive way she regarded as her own. In three thousand years, the Colegio, its cement blocks and pressed wood paneling would be gone, along with its *papier maché* artifacts but these rock piles would remain, she thought, and people would wonder.

He came, at ten, through the coleus border, and stood beside her, a short man, no taller than she but big, with a chest like a bull and a large head beginning to bald at the temples.

"You must not walk through the gardens," she said, not looking at him. He laughed, "Hello, Warsaw..." But the children overran the moment. She glared them into silence and left. There was time, all the time they needed.

She drank a cup of coffee in the lounge, ate the corn pancake with white cheese from the hotel, then corrected three or four of the science tests before discovering she'd forgotten her grade book. Returning to get it, she crossed the grass again, to the open side of her classroom. When she walked in, Ordóñez, who was talking excitedly, was sitting on the edge of her classroom desk.

Instead of entering, she sat on the rim of the tile floor to listen. Two of the children saw her, but she put her finger to her lips. Ordóñez did not notice her; he was talking rapidly, mixing English and Spanish. "...my contention is that the ideas of Rousseau have been applied but once, and that was on a sugar plantation outside Caracas..."

Rousseau? she wondered, whatever happened to *"La Cucaracha"*?

"...laughed at today," he went on, "his 'Noble Savage.' Well, if the savage turned out not so noble, the idea was a noble one. Yes, let the child run naked, let him touch, taste, sniff the world..." Here, Ordóñez leaped off the desk, pantomiming these actions, flaring his nostrils. The children shrieked, sensing some dangerous skirting of the rules.

"He had an ideal pupil, Rousseau," he reclaimed their attention, "Emile was the name he gave this pupil."

Emile? she wondered. These are fifth graders. What are they going to know of Emile?

"He wrote a book about him, this Emile," Ordóñez went on, "but he never found him in life..."

"Ha! but there was this other young man who found him." Ordóñez glared at them.

"Oh, you are ignorant. It is not your fault, but you are snotnoses, ignorant of history!" The children shrieked in delight at this insult. "Well, I must remedy your ignorance. Listen, this other young man, Simón Rodríguez, reader of Rousseau, found his Emile, his ideal pupil: his name was Simón Bolívar, son of wealthy Creoles, there on a sugar plantation outside Caracas..."

She thought of that exercise book open on the floor that night: *"Simón Bolívar, as a child ran naked as a..."*

"Yes, two Simóns," he went on. "One a wanderer, schoolmaster, candle maker, reader of Rousseau and the other, a wild boy, orphaned, undisciplined, the despair of his uncles: the uncles turned him over to Rodríguez. Simón Rodríguez became young Simón Bolívar's tutor, set him sniffing, exploring this dewy new world, fragrant with humus, mosses, mountain streams..." Here he waved his arms out toward the mountains, looked right at her and didn't see her. The children were beginning to giggle behind their hands. Enrique Fensterberg, his eyes dancing, was standing on his chair in order to see better. How would it end? She was filled with fear.

"Liberty!" Ordóñez shouted. "This Simón Rodríguez taught young Simón Bolívar to love liberty! But..." Enrique Fensterberg fell into his seat. "But another young man who was being educated about this same time would bring him low...

"Yes, snotnoses," Ordóñez spoke quietly now, "Yes, you snotnoses, this other infant was wrapped in wool from birth, as was the custom in those chilly, theological mountains of New Granada. His limbs were bound, his education overlooked by priests. His name was, ahem..." here he put on a pompous air: "Francisco de Paula Santander. Born in Cúcuta, the border between the two colonies, a Man of Borders, you shall see...

"Imagine it, now. They're both grown. The second, Francisco de Paula, is a young seminarian in Santafé. It is the year 1811. The colonies are in an uproar. Our young seminarian has heard noises about Independence, and turned soldier. His uncle, the priest, has obtained a commission for him in the militia of New Granada, but..."Ordóñez held up a finger. "But is he ready for a battle? Ah, that is a matter for some thought. Yes, some thought. A battle is a serious thing..." He mopped his face with his handkerchief. It was a hot day for such exertion.

"So, we find him writing a letter to his uncle the priest: "'Respected Uncle,' he writes, 'Our unit marches south the week to come. As you know...post of Standard Bearer you secured me...one of gravest risk to one of my small knowledge of military arts...beg you not leap to conclusion your nephew a coward. On day they ran the Viceroy from his house I was among the first, to which *Fulano* can attest...' Notice," Ordóñez said, "how he must always have a witness to his so-called courage but, to go on, at this gallant action, he tells his uncle, he was bruised, no wounded, wounded! And at Lomapelada, at Lomapelada a bullet entered a post on which his hand was resting, ha ha! A post on which his hand was resting...

"So we have him, our hero. He isn't afraid; he is the hero of Lomapelada. But he will not go south with his unit, as he hasn't yet learned military arts to his satisfaction." Ordóñez paced, a finger in the air.

"But he is a master of other arts. The art of covering his tracks. This is the first of many letters, memoirs, excuses, the 'Memoir Writer,' they called him. The 'Soldier of the Pen.'" He stopped in his tracks and glared at the children. "Why do I tell you about this abyss of a man? You," he pointed to Enrique, "You, tell me why I bother with this sneak, this coward?"

Enrique was speechless.

"Ha, you are ignorant. You are the most ignorant children I have ever run across!"

They screamed with pleasure at this. Billy Ostertag tipped over in his chair. Dorie stood up, appalled, but Ordóñez shouted them down. "You," he ordered Enrique, "look him up for us in the *Encyclopedia Britannica* there. Santander,

• 27 •

Francisco de Paula!" Enrique went and got the volume out of the lower shelves, and fumbled through the pages. Ordóñez went over and roughly found it for him. They're only little children, Dorie thought, why must he...?

"Read it," Ordóñez ordered, and Enrique stood up and read.

"'Liberator of the colony of New Granada. Father of the Republic of...'"

"You see," shouted Ordóñez, "where his pen got him!" His possessed gaze swept over her and the children again, without even seeing her.

"AND how is your *Americanita*?" Ricaurte asked Ordóñez that afternoon when they were alone in the teachers' lounge. "I had suggested to you an 'arrangement,' but have reconsidered. You should marry her. Listen, I have a nephew..."

Ricaurte had many nephews, all of them illustrations of some virtue or vice or another.

"...married his English instructor at the Language Institute, a girl from Texas. He was a miserable clerk at the time for a stationers...sold pens and pencils, but ambitious, not like his brother Alfonso who..."

"Yes, yes," Ordóñez said, impatient. He was having trouble with the ditto machine, which someone had left in the on-ink position.

"So, he was taking these English courses, and had this instructor...pretty girl, but not especially young...and thick legs. My God! I never saw such legs. Ran in her family, I suppose, and you never see them on our women..."

Ordóñez was getting an echo on his ditto master.

"Anyway," Ricaurte went on. "He started asking her out.

He was poor, but good-looking, the rascal and, after all, she wasn't so young anymore and with those legs...So, they took up together, married, and moved back to Texas. You see what I'm getting at, man?"

Ordóñez shrugged.

"Listen, as this girl's husband, he obtained a green card like that!" Ricaurte snapped his fingers in Ordóñez's face.

"My dear Ricaurte, what does all this have to do with me?"

"Man, a green card! A green card is the entry to everything! You know if you were to go there unsponsored, as it were, in order to obtain a green card you must first establish a skill that..."

"Ricaurte!"

"...Frenchman I knew, spoke three languages, went off there to live, applied for a green card. The authorities were required to run an ad in all the major newspapers for a person with those accomplishments, those three languages. If one person answered that ad, he would be disqualified."

"Ricaurte!"

"...he would be taking the employment of one of their citizens. So, you see the impossibility..."

"Ricaurte, I was not thinking of going to Texas or..."

"Now the Señorita West is no longer so very young. Her legs are acceptable, but reflect the tendency of her race..."

"Ricaurte, you will please show some respect for..."

"I am merely concerned for your..."

"I was not thinking of going to Texas or securing any green..."

"Your well-being and your family are..."

"...any green card, in the first place! And in the second, he was not thinking of marrying..." Ordóñez had rolled a master into the typewriter and was retyping his open letter to the parents of his students. "I am grieving, Ricaurte. Why don't *you* marry Miss West? To my mind she is a fine person, and very attractive."

"Ah, you know my affliction," Ricaurte murmured.

"For a green card, perhaps you can, shall we say, overcome your..."

"You don't understand."

"No, I don't, and neither do you. My point is, I respect your affliction. Can you not respect mine?"

"Ah, well, it is just for your own good, I think. If you cannot love her, think what it could mean to the children. She would be a good mother to them..."

Ordóñez typed his fateful letter, not listening.

When he came to her classroom the next day, she exited through the hall door and made a circuit of the building coming back by way of the lawn and sitting again on the border of the tile floor where the garden bloomed. She didn't understand why she was doing this.

He began today teaching them a song in Spanish.

"Twenty-five Frenchmen
To pull his cannon,
Alon alon camina
Alon mozos alon."

They sang it madly, three times through before Ordóñez shushed them.

"They were singing that in 1811 because our Simón—The Man from Caracas, they called him—had brought back the revolutionary, Miranda, from France. He was old by then, Napoleon's friend, Miranda. In his ear he wore a gold hoop, ha ha! A hoop he'd wear in hell, they said. They were going to fight the Spaniards *à la mode française, la la!*" Ordóñez

• 30 •

did a little mincing jig. The children looked warily at Dorie for a moment, then threw themselves under his spell, screaming with laughter until he shouted them down.

"But no it wasn't to be! Napoleon's old friend found nothing in this benighted place but swamps and mosquitoes. Royalist mosquitoes, ha! There was no support for Don Simón's war because creoles, mulattos, black slaves, even the mosquitoes, were royalists. They wouldn't fight. And, even if they did, it wouldn't be in the 'French style.' He forgot what it was like here, Miranda, with his military arts, his officers from France. Our ragtag army of half-breeds, what had they to do with him?"

"Twenty-five mulattos
To pull his cannon
Alon, alon, camina
Alon, mozos, alon!"

He allowed them to scream it again at the top of their lungs.

"And so," he went on, perspiring heavily now, "Our Miranda surrendered right at the start, according to the best military etiquette, of course, *la la*!"

"*La la*," the children shouted: "*La la*!"

"...tried to sneak aboard a British ship. They captured him, though, and threw him in prison.

"That was the last of his idols. He never had another. He stood naked, naked before his creator." He spoke softly now. Enrique stood still in the middle of the aisle where he'd been prancing.

"There was a terrible earthquake. In Caracas. There came a terrifying rumble. The earth opened. Again, and again, the terrible roar. The people ran into the streets. We perish!" Ordóñez shouted, holding his head.

"There, it comes again!" He pounded on the desk "Take cover! Quick, it comes again!" He swept her books to the floor.

No, no he mustn't excite them so. She stood up.

"The priests climbed on the piles of rubble...He mounted the chair...and preached judgment on a wicked people that conspired to throw over that most benevolent of monarchs, Fernando the Seventh! The people fell at the feet of the priests. 'Father, give me confession!' 'Father, forgive me.' On the day my sainted wife died, I went to the cockfights. 'Father, marry me to this woman I've lived with in sin for twenty years...' "

He was leaping about, kneeling, groveling, playing all roles.

"When, suddenly, the priest caught sight of *him* with his ragged army, helping drag people out from under the rubble. 'There he is!' cried Padre Lamota, 'It is he who has caused the earth to open, who has brought this judgment upon us! He and the devil Miranda he has brought us from France! Kneel!' he ordered Bolívar. 'Kneel, blasphemer! Repent conspiracies against that most virtuous of kings!'

"'Repent, I will not!'" Ordóñez cried, relishing his impersonation of Bolívar.

"And throwing down the priest. 'Nature, Nature conspires with Despotism against us,' Bolívar shouts. 'Well, then, we'll take on Nature, too, and bend her will to ours!'"

"No!" she cried, standing up. The children, all out of their seats, stared at her. "You mustn't excite them so!"

"Ah, Miss West," he wiped his face. "I didn't see you there. I was just enacting for them..."

"Yes, yes, I saw. It is wonderful. It is fine, fine, but they can't possibly comprehend..."

"Comprehend?"

She became confused. "I'm sorry. I shouldn't have interrupted. Please, please pardon me and go on. I was afraid they might become too excited and disturb other classes." Actually it had been in her mind he might draw down Mr. Hillyer's displeasure. There was some talk of a dispute between the principal and the Spanish teachers, something about a petition. If he didn't fear for his job, she did. She had seen his poverty.

"Please, go on," she said. But to her immense relief the bell rang.

THURSDAY morning, she had a note in her box, calling her into Mr. Hillyer's office.

"Yes, Miss West," he said, pointing her to a sling chair, which threw her into a rather awkward position. He was not a very intimidating man, she thought. He was slightly shorter than she and boyish-looking, besides, with lank black hair that fell over his forehead but he was a bit of a martinet, able to go from amiability to sudden anger, perhaps because of his youth and fear of insubordination. He was a Mormon from Salt Lake City, and rather moralistic for her taste. "This Ordóñez," he began, "Are you aware of what is going on in his classes?"

"No," she lied. "I usually go out when he comes in."

"Usually," he picked up. "So you are there sometimes?"

"Well, yes," she admitted.

"And what have you observed these times?"

"Why do you ask?"

"Well," he tapped a sheaf of papers on his desk, "There are matters that have come to my attention, which I am not to…And also passing the back of your classroom today, I couldn't help noticing that it was a bit noisy, and that Mr. Ordóñez was standing on a desk."

"Oh, no," she said. "Mr. Ordóñez becomes a bit excited, but he has never stood on a desk. A chair, perhaps, but..."

"But," he interrupted, "you say you are not usually there."

"Well..." She was a little angry now, and tried to get out of the sling chair. "If you must know, I am usually there lately, but I wasn't aware I was supposed to stay there..."

"No, of course, you are not," he said. "It is your break Why *are* you there? I'm wondering."

"That is my concern," she said shortly, "seeing it is my break."

"Miss West, of course it's your concern. My intention was to discover if you've noted anything at any time you happened to be there—returning a bit early, perhaps—if you've noted anything. You say he becomes a bit excited, for example..."

"Mr. Ordóñez is very excited by his subject," she said.

"And what is that subject?"

"He's telling them about Simón Bolívar," she said. She saw nothing to conceal about his subject. The *Colegio* was named for The Liberator, after all.

"Are you aware that Mr. Ordóñez has a curriculum to follow?" he said.

"No," she said. "I hadn't thought about it. He seems to me an exceptionally well-educated man, certainly qualified to establish his own curriculum."

"Mr. Ordóñez was consulted about the curriculum a year ago. It was read over and initialed by him." Mr. Hillyer picked up the very curriculum from his desk and was about to hand it to her for her inspection. She waved it away.

"I just don't think this is any of my business," she said,

annoyed. "And what I happen to observe when I'm not required to be there should not be held against another teacher. None of us go strictly by a curriculum and I don't recall ever initialing such a thing. Why should Mr. Ordóñez? Can't they learn a little Spanish by hearing about this man the school is named after, after all, as well from anything else?"

"Miss West, it is the principle."

Yes, she saw it was, and that she was just making things worse for her poor friend. She got up from the chair. Mr. Hillyer was a man to chase principle down the narrowest streets. Not a bad man. It was he who had instituted the half hour of Spanish a day, and who had recruited the two Spanish teachers. Still, she left feeling bad and used. If she hadn't been so caught off-guard, she could have stood on principle herself, and refused to say anything at all about what went on during her break.

Wednesday, when Mr. Ordóñez came, Miss West was at her post again.

"Do the earthquake again," the children clamored but he was subdued, serious.

"Ah no, snotnoses, time is short…"

Short? she wondered, but we have all the time we…

"Short, my children. Recall, now, our seminarian, he wouldn't go. He wrote that letter, remember? And, after all, the affair wasn't so dangerous: six wounded on our side, none killed and all who went received promotions. He'd be a colonel now.

"Well, now there's a plot being hatched against the president. Spanish troops stand on the border and Santafé must defend itself against its own congress. This period is known as the 'Foolish Fatherland.' Our seminarian takes part this time. He is gloriously captured by the women of Santafé and scratched in the face, ha ha!

"But beware of humiliated men, my children. They are the most dangerous, yes! Remember this...

"Meanwhile, *he* has come, our Simón. Out of the rubble of his Caracas, he's brought this ragged, beggarly army to impose his bloody plots on this peaceable land of New Granada, which not a drop of Spanish blood has yet stained. What need has New Granada of these savages from across the border? *He* didn't see borders, you understand.

"'It's blood he wants,' they squealed, these timid New Granadans. Yes, blood!

"'He'll do away with the congress!' they cried. They were obsessed with congresses. They all wanted their turn at legislating and no one saw that war must come. They must have leaders."

He's mad, thought Dorie. They're only little children. All this took place a hundred-fifty years ago, and he's talking as if it were yesterday.

"And meanwhile, though ordered not to try it, Bolívar chased the Spaniards out of the lower Magdalena valley with barely two hundred men. The dispatches they receive in Santafé are signed 'The Liberator. '

"The Liberator, yes. It's always been a quality of great men that they are conscious of who they are! Yes! ha!" He paced in front of the dismayed children, a finger in the air.

"And Francisco de Paula, saw it. 'This man's the future,' he said. Santander was a coward and a traitor, but he saw...

"And so he throws in his lot with the Man from Caracas. He's sent to Cúcuta to be Castillo's second-in-command. The Spaniards on the border can no longer be ignored. They're with our Simón now. Castillo, Torres, Garcia..." He was talking rapidly, in Spanish and in English, sketching a map on the blackboard and dotting it with a broken piece of chalk..." With him but at every turn betraying, bothering him like gnats around his head. He asks for troops, supplies and they withhold them. Francisco de Paula sends word that his men desert: 'One cannot blame them, they have no rations, no pay,' writes Sergeant Major Santander, 'Nowhere in the world are soldiers asked to serve under these conditions...' Ha!"

He seized a paper from her desk and crumpled it, "But, if this was a *war like no other that had ever been!*

"And Bolívar writes.

"'Send orders! We march immediately! To Caracas! If we stay here, we will sink into Sergeant Major Santander's slough. '

"But, again, he wouldn't go. His orders from the congress were to protect the region around Cúcuta. His men deserted, there was nothing to eat, and so...

"He didn't go. He didn't go, and the others marched, triumphant, into Caracas...

"*A war like no other,* my children. Every cavalryman carried two foot-soldiers behind on the rump of his horse. What a sight it must have been. Ah, yes! They entered Caracas, victorious, and there were 'beautiful women and glorious medals and we were fired by love,' he writes, my black-eyed Simón.

"And for that other, Francisco de Paula, it was a bad moment. He must explain in his memoirs why he didn't go with Bolívar, yes..." Ordóñez sat down, here, and mopped his brow, "And these 'explanations' found their way into our history books and into the speeches of our statesmen, et cetera et cetera, and into *those,* for example." He waved toward the encyclopedias, "so that Ordóñez must exert himself in this heat to save you snotnoses from this vast..."

He had lost them, she saw. April Cornfeld and Lupita Esperanza were huddled together filling in their math workbooks.

"Veinticinco franceses!" Enrique Fensterberg shouted, with one nervous glance at her, and Ordóñez let them sing it.

"Veinticinco franceses arrastran su cañon.

Alón alón camina..."

Which was a fortunate circumstance, for Mr. Hillyer was just at that moment going down the path that separated the two primary school buildings. He was known to approve of the singing of little songs in Spanish classes, and could have no knowledge of the inflammatory nature of this one.

But why am I standing guard over him like this, she wondered. It's none of my...She stepped into the classroom just as the bell was ringing. "Mr. Ordóñez, I..." But the children were still shouting out the chorus.

"Alón, alón, camina..."

"That will do!" she cried, and they were silent. "Mr. Ordóñez, I, I've become quite taken up by all of this. I mean I've quite enjoyed...and I thank you for allowing me to stay... but don't you think...I...I mean they are just children..."

"Children, yes. They are our resource, did you ever consider that, Miss West? This sixty percent of your school which is the native population, they are our future professional people, our scholars, our governing class."

"Yes, yes," she nodded.

"Most of them can barely write a sentence in their native language. They know nothing of our history. Or what little they know is false, false!"

"Yes, I can see..."

"So I must use this little space. I must rant and perspire..." He mopped his face. The children were listless in their seats.

"But it isn't enough!" He waved a sheaf of papers in his hand, handing her one. "Read this."

"Sixty percent of the day...to correspond to sixty percent of school population..." she read, becoming alarmed, "...devoted to instruction in their native language...history, literature of own..."

"And what is this?" she asked. "Who is it for?"

"A letter," he said, "to be sent to parents and trustees..."

"No, no!" she cried.

"Is it not well expressed? I was just going to duplicate it on the..."

"It is expressed perfectly well, but you cannot, you must not...!" She was thinking of that half-built house, the dusty leatherette chairs, the pictures taped crookedly..."Mr. Ordóñez!"

He was smiling at her. "You took yourself off the other morning. I did not behave in a very seemly...perhaps we might attempt another..."

She was filled with confusion, staring at the seditious letter. Time, all the time in the world, was reduced to the few days it would take for this letter to be copied and sent.

"I'm afraid," she said.

"One mustn't be afraid. One must be a little brave sometimes, my dear *Señorita* West," he said.

"So," he began Thursday when he came again, "They were all heroes in Caracas, while he, Francisco de Paula, was stuck in Cúcuta. It was rumored the city would be sacked..."

Sitting again on the edge of the classroom where the bougainvillea grew, she wondered if the letter had been sent and, if so, how long it would take before the trustees...

"But, 'Take heart,' his compatriots tell our traitor, our 'Soldier of the Pen.' 'Things begin to look ugly for Don Simón. The Spaniards have regained control of the plains.'" He drew another hasty map, breaking his chalk and flinging it away into the coleus border.

"The tide is turning in favor of the congress. Don Simón is excommunicated by Francisco de Paula's uncle. In Santafé they arm even the Spaniards against him. 'He is ours,' Garcia tells Santander. 'He cannot win without us and if he loses...'

"And *He*," Ordóñez shouted at the dreamy children who would be the governing class, thought Dorie with a smile.

"And *He*, Bolívar, what can he do? These men, they support him with their words. Yet they are worse than the enemy. An enemy, he could attack, but these men...

"Patience, though, for time is an ally. Time allows the Spaniards to besiege Cartagena, and then what use are congresses? Yes!" He paced back and forth in front of the bemused children. "This land, these mountains, who but he dreamed of what might arise from them? This blood, shed and mingled: Creole, Mulatto, Black...A new race, taking possession of a CONTINENT!"

What will happen to him? Dorie wondered. He'll never find another post in the middle of the school year...

"They," Ordóñez continued, his eyes on Enrique, "Santander and his cronies, dreamed only of congresses, of republics: Venezuela, Ecuador...of a turn at being president..."

What will his children do? his sister? she wondered.

"But patience! He will wait. He can wait and so the Spaniards surround them..." He attempted another map, broke another piece of chalk and flung it away.

His pockets must always be full of chalk, and his jackets always covered with chalk dust, Dorie thought, depressed. Impossible to be any poorer then he is, and he's worried about...

"...Calzada in Pamplona, Sámano in the South. They enter Santafé. Imagine market stalls abandoned, as dogs run off with the meat, chickens run loose in the plaza, miscarriages, ah! The army has fled to the swamps of Casanare, carrying the Virgin of Chiquinquirá like the Ark of Covenant...

"Lost, snotnoses, all is lost. But all has been lost before, will be again!" he cried. The children were riveted not only by the queer tale, but, by the queerness of it all: their teacher remaining at the edge of the classroom, Ordóñez seeming to forget that they were even there, until he fixed them with his gaze and said quietly.

"Neither of them ever gave up. The Man from Caracas, the Man from Cúcuta.

"Bolívar kept trying to take Caracas. But Caracas was not what was needed. What was needed was southward, inward, wild heart. Ah, snotnoses..." He broke another piece of chalk on his map. Dorie looked at the children. They were grinning at each other. He'd lost them again, the 'future ruling class.' Only she was listening.

He went on as if possessed.

"Trinidad de Arichuna! God's oven! Imagine it. A shack over there..." He waved his arms around the room. "And that's the presidential palace! But where else could it be, if Spaniards held all the rest?

"What a fate, snotnoses, what a fate to be left nothing but Trinidad de Arichuna! The New Granadans lie around in ragged shorts, fanning themselves, while the Venezuelan cowboys round up wild horses. And the Memoir Writer has shut himself up in his tent. The horses die of hunger, his men accuse him, and he does nothing. What would they have him do? Wrestle crocodiles? Attack the enemy with a whittled stick?"

And why am I listening to this? she asked herself. This has nothing to do with me. Impossible to be any poorer than Ordóñez. She thought again of the house at Cuarta Bis, the pages from *Good Housekeeping* taped crookedly to the walls.

"They laugh at him, a man who's useless in this wild place. But do they think Santander lies there with his head empty? Do they think he doesn't see these cowboys creating bad blood between Granadans and Venezuelans? Or that the men want the brute Páez in his place? He sees it well. A civilized man cannot lead savages. They want the brute Páez, they shall have him. What does he care about their wild horses? He has a plan. He will humble himself before this illiterate cowboy.

"So, again, humiliated. Beware of humiliated men, snotnoses. They are the most dangerous.

"Savagery, treachery. Officers are murdered for a bit of loot. Morillo comes with five-thousand men. It is madness to stay here. There is nothing else to do. The Memoir Writer will seek him, suffer his vanity. He goes to Bolívar."

…the naked light bulb, the dusty chairs…no, it is impossible…

"Meanwhile, my children, *he* has arrived, my black-eyed Simón, come from the islands with ships, arms, a printing press. The Spaniards hold all the ports, so they land in

Guyana, build a port there.

"And they meet again, The Man from Caracas, The Man from…

"Cúcuta, you wouldn't march…' " Bolívar recalls.

"I mean to change your opinion," the other says," Ordóñez was playing all the roles.

"Well, the Man from Caracas relents. Santander's to have his opportunity. They'll return together. There's no way back but through The Man from Caracas. They all see it.

"But it's Santafé he should be thinking of, not Caracas. Venezuela's ruined. Eight years of war, the harvest unreaped. And in Caracas, they call him crazy: *El Loco Simón*. No man is a prophet in his own…

"But New Granada's rich, untouched, arid if he were to attack its capital, who would expect it? Look, look out there. "Ordóñez waved toward the mountains. "How many of you snotnoses have ever crossed it?"

Robbie Plimford, the Vice Consul's son, raised his hand.

"What did you cross it in?"

"A Landrover."

"How long did it take you?"

"A day and a half."

"How would you like to cross it on foot, your feet wrapped in rags? Eh? They are going to attack Santafé," he went on "Who would believe it possible to head a hand of barefoot plainsmen through those passes, over that mountain range? Impossible!"

The bell rang. She stepped in through the garden.

"Ah, Miss West…"

"The letter, did you send it?" she asked.

"Yesterday," he said. "It's done. What happens, happens."

• 43 •

"And your job here?"

"Ah, Ordóñez is one for flinging away jobs. So, you are still attending my little lectures?"

"Yes, yes," she said. "When I first came here, I looked at those mountains. We drove up as far as La Colmena, and I remember thinking how those mountains must do things to people, must work on them in extraordinary ways…"

"Yes, yes! His buttocks—you will pardon the expression, my dear *Señorita*—Bolívar's buttocks, it was said, were worn to calluses from crossing and recrossing those slopes on mule back. "."

"I hope you don't mind my…"

"Ah, no," he said. "I speak now to you as well as to them. You are the best listener."

We are so formal, she thought, recalling that evening when they worked at her buttons.

"Yes," he said. "These are most elevated matters. When I think about them, I am proud. I am a man. I can do what I could not the other night…"

She smiled, her face dappled with the sunlight filtered through the vines.

"Such an incompetent thief," he said. "It was a shameful affair all around. You have not been walking about the streets in your costume again, I trust."

"No, I'm quite myself again," she laughed.

66 NATURE, nature defended those passes. No need of Spaniards," he told the children Thursday.

She sat in her usual place, gazing out at "those passes." The snowcap was uncovered today, pink in sunlight, above a bank of bruised clouds.

"No, they wouldn't be defended, those passes but how

to drive those lowlanders up and over? It was time for them to repair their roofs after the rains of February and March. But most of them, snotnoses, no longer had any roofs. There hadn't been a harvest in two years. Their cattle had been driven off by the Spaniards...

"He promised them Sogamoso, that rich high plain, with wheat fields, orchards...but how to galvanize them? These petty rivalries were tearing them apart. Páez conspires in Apure, with Santander under his nose. My Simón cannot put a finger on it. They want less, and they'll outlast him. Every night he burns with fever. Time is on their side; they dream small dreams. Returning from these wars, they'll take their turns in congress, raise their children, and die in bed with priests around...

"And he, alone, with no wife, no child. He doubts himself at times. Is it some misteaching then, this glory of arms? Something that has never been, or passing? Just some mistake?

"No! he has spun out glory, felt it at his back, his front..."

How can I not care for this man? she thinks...

"No, my Simón has merely lost himself a moment. Oh those swamps, those wild vastnesses, how they darken vision..."

This exasperating man?

"Listen, snotnoses, he's sent a spy, a priest in disguise, to see how things are, off there in New Granada. There are many rumors of patriots hanged and quartered, rumors that sentiment there runs in his favor and, at this dark moment, a messenger appears, reports on the execution of one 'La Pola,' accused of smuggling arms to patriots in Apure. She was said to have been very beautiful, 'La Pola.' A great crowd had gathered to see her executed. They questioned her in public: Was it true that she contrived to send arms?

"It was true.

"And would she give names of her accomplices?

"She would give no names.

"And so she was sentenced to the firing squad. They offered her wine and she refused.

"'I will have nothing from the hands of tyrants,' she cried.

"And had she anything else to say before? they asked, and she replied. 'He comes who will avenge my death!'

"And they fired six shots into her tender breast, then cut off her head. Ah, yes, when *he*, Bolívar, heard this, it was decided that they would liberate Santafé..."

Lupita Virgas had her hand up. Was all this *true*?

"Ah, yes, there was such heroism and often it was women," said Ordóñez.

"For it was well known that he was soft on women and they on him. Often, when he entered a city, the maidens dressed themselves in white, and flung flowers in his path. Ah, snotnoses, he was very human. We can love this man...

"And so it was decided. They would scale the central range of the Andes and fall on Santafé. There were good, tactical reasons for this decision: whoever held New Granada held the center, divided the Spanish..."

Ordóñez sketched a hasty map, broke his chalk, and the bell sounded.

"Half an hour," he complained to her. "What can one accomplish in half an hour?" he was irritated and distracted today.

"They have turned me down Warsaw," he said. Her heart thumped. "And, also, I am to stick to the curriculum. So

I shall, but one more half hour is needed. You shall see. Ordóñez shall go out in a blaze of glory like 'La Pola.' la la!"

SHE decided to put him out of her mind. That carnival night was a passing fling. That she happened to see him daily had nothing to do with his feelings or intentions. And even that contact would soon be ended. It was like pulling in a runaway horse by now to stop her feelings, but she set out to attempt it. She would hear the end of the story; it couldn't take much longer. She and Feli had even had a sober conversation about the perils of such intercultural relationships.

"What did he have to work with?" he began Friday. The brute Páez, the serpent Santander, a motley of lowlanders on wild ponies that sickened on the unfamiliar grass and split their hooves. But he will use them all; he will use all, and bend their will to his purpose.

"And Santander? He also has a plan. One uses and is used, snotnoses but the man who has a plan uses all men, even the greatest. Ah yes. Santander's worked his way into the good graces of the Liberator and has been sent to pacify the factions in Apure, to get the Granadans to fight alongside Venezuelans. He plans to do no such thing, of course," Ordóñez glared at the children. "Remember all I've told you about this man now. His aims are little ones: to get back there to his pleasant colony he needs Bolívar, but once he gets there it is for him and his likes to administer—they are still there, he and his likes, administering it, in Bogotá, Caracas...

"But the present problem: how to drive them up and over? It comes to my Simón one day. Listen. Santander is on his way to Apure. A letter of his is intercepted and brought to Bolívar.

• 47 •

"We Granadans must unite in throwing off the yoke of these strutting prideful Venezuelans. Ha! The Soldier of the Pen has gotten himself in trouble now!

"Have him detained at the mouth of the Meta,' my Simón orders. And then it comes to him, his grand scheme: 'No!' he cries. He's changed his mind. 'Let him go. Let Páez deal with him as he wishes.'"

Ordóñez raised a finger. "Do you see it? He let it be: that antagonistic energy is what would drive them up and over!

"But let us go on. Time is short." He looked at the clock, drew another map. "May 28, they camp in Hato Guerreno; May 31, in Mata de Valentin; June 2, Guasdalito; June 10, all day, all night, crossing the Lupa River. 'His eyes,' said Páez, 'who could resist his eyes!' Cúcuta, then, the mountains. These plainsmen have their first look at our Andes. A wall, it seems to them, a monstrous, dripping, mossy wall, hung straight from heaven! Their horses begin to die; they have no shoes; their feet are wrapped in rags. Many desert but he keeps promising them this golden land of Sogamoso, and letting the divisions widen, the bad blood work. As they approach the summit, he divides them into two forces: Granadan and Venezuelan, encourages them to compete, insult each other. Horses die, Men fall and lay down in the snow to die. He calls his generals together: 'Gentlemen, the enterprise is a perilous one; half or more of us may die of hunger and cold. What do you say? Shall we turn back?' Ah, snotnoses, this man is a supreme student of human nature.

"Páez, of course, says 'Go on,' and Santander, what can he say but, 'If he can do it, I can!' And all of them: 'We Granadans won't be outdone by any puffed-up Venezuelans.'

"'Well, then, Gentlemen, you've decided,'" Bolívar tells them. "You see now, snotnoses, why he set them in competition, how it falls together? Yes, yes! They're wondering which pass he'll use. It's rumored it'll be Labragranza. No, say others, Paya." He reveals it now. "It's Pisba."

"Pisba!"

"No one comes through Pisba! Who'd believe it? Not the Spaniards. There's not a troop in sight! And so, they go on. Those who make it," Ordóñez was talking rapidly now, his eyes on the clock, "Those who make it return for others, bringing food, clothing, horses.

"The rest you ought to know that they surprised the Spaniards. This man was Father, Father of America!

"They captured the center and Santander said: 'Bolívar wanted to turn back. I dissuaded him. You are my witnesses. He'll have the glory, when it was I...'"

The bell rang. "Go on," she mouthed the words, remaining in her place.

"Yes, he put it in his infernal memoirs, this Santander," Ordóñez continued. "'It was I who persuaded him; I am the Liberator of New Granada,' he wrote."

"But never mind. It held the vision of Sogamoso in those days, Boyacá. My Simón held the center, went south: Ecuador, Peru. It fell apart behind him, into their hands: Páez, Santander. They divided it between them, those men of borders: New Granada to Santander, Venezuela to Páez. And my Simón, he died consumed..." Ordóñez looked at her. "Go on, go on," she said, keeping her place.

"Went out like a woodspark. Alone, but for an English doctor in attendance. They all outlived him, fathered children, served as President of the Republic: Venezuela, Ecuador..."

Go on, go on, she nodded at him.

"The vision was betrayed, snotnoses but it's there for those who'll see it, even now: Indian, Creole, Black...a vig-

• 49 •

orous new race, taking possession of a continent, a continent! It's there for you to seize onto, ha! You!

"Ah, snotnoses," he shook his bead ruefully, "I am a schoolteacher, and have this habit of instructing snotnoses. I am like him, Simón Rodríguez. Remember him. The man who taught my Simón. After *he* died—his Emile—Rodríguez became a wanderer. He wandered over this continent, founding a school here and there, a candle factory beside it. And, everywhere, he put up a sign which read.

'American Lights and Virtues

Wax candles, Patience, Soap,

Resignation, Head erect,

And Love of Work.'"

He paused with his finger in the air. "I thank you, Miss West," he said to her with a slight bow in her direction.

She came into the room.

"I have finished and I am grateful to you, as I said," he told her as he walked toward the door.

"But..."

"I am to stick to the curriculum in the future," he said, and went out.

On Monday, Miss West decided to not attend his lesson. He had greeted her so politely she thought he must be angry. Suddenly she was shy with him. In spite of all her resolve, she loved him, even if she never saw him again. She had never felt this way.

He was gone when she returned, a poem left behind on her blackboard. She allowed it to remain and, when the children were gone, copied it into her notebook and tried to do a translation. Poetry ought to be beyond her, she knew, but she welcomed the struggle after the inanities with busboys at the hotel. It seemed a difficult poem for fifth graders. Had he put it there for her? Or for himself?

BEFORE he came on Tuesday, she copied her lines on the blackboard. The Bolívar story was over. When she returned, the children were busy writing something, and no one dared to say a word.

She gestured toward the blackboard "I made…this," she said when he came in and stood beside her.

"And Earth returns, with its birds…"

He read her words aloud. He seemed distracted and had an envelope in his hand with the school letterhead.

'It's the poem you left," she said.

"Ah, yes…"

"It caused me a great deal of trouble. I didn't know about the word '*acontece*'. I tried 'Earth accomplishes with its birds…"

"Yes it is difficult. The Earth is, how do you express it? Punctual?"

"Yes. Punctual."

"It accomplishes its tasks with great regularity, and it returns punctually, but where there is one word to say both in Spanish, in English there are two."

"It is a fine poem," she said.

"Yes, yes! It's a fine poem." He was looking at her in the manner, she remembered, that he had looked at her when he told her about his wife's death.

'The poet couldn't sleep, and the dawn came…" He stared down at the envelope in his hand. She thought he would open it then, but he didn't.

"Who wrote it?" she asked.

"A young man. He lives, now, in Mexico; he is well

known there, but hardly thought of here. Out poets cannot live here..." He shook his large head as if bothered by an insect. "Everything, we import everything: Scotch whiskey, unimucks, frozen green peas, schools. Our poets, we export...

"Unless they are very bad poets," he added, "And then we make them president..."

"I don't understand. Is President Vallezuela a poet?"

"Like all of them. Some have been good poets, novelists. Not this one. I ask myself, which is worse, the poetry, or the administration? I think the poetry. He is a writer of sonnets in the Italian manner. His father was an essayist. He was president also, once before El Cacique, once after..." He frowned, then looked down at the white envelope in his hand. "A man of letters...Ha! We are all men of letters! Ordóñez included. Ordóñez has a disease of filling pages with words..."

She was silent, bewildered.

"But I must open this," he said.

"What is it?" she asked. He looked so shaken.

He took a knife from his pocket, slit the envelope and handed her the letter inside.

"But what is it?" She feared suddenly for all the mornings.

"Read, read it to me," he ordered her hoarsely.

She read:

As of today, your duties as teacher of Spanish in the
elementary grades are terminated.
W. Hillyer

"But why? Why?" she cried. The children were whispering now. Lupita was giggling.

"So...so. It is what I thought," he said.

"What is the reason?" she persisted.

"It is the disease of filling pages with words..." He held his hand out for the letter.

"I am so sorry!" she cried.

"Thank you, Miss West," he said, and left the room.

So much for the intercultural relationship. She was grateful for the tentative beginnings at drawing herself up. It helped that she didn't see him. The next day it was Ricaurte who came through the garden to teach the children "La Cucaracha."

She asked Ricaurte how his friend fared.

'Ah, Ordóñez, he attracts bad luck!"

"What will he do?"

'He has found work."

"I'm glad about that!"

"At the Villegas Academy he is teaching sixty sons of laundresses.

"But it is work," she said.

"Twelve hundred and sixty pesos a month. A pair of shoes costs two thousand. He will earn a shoe a month."

There were rainstorms out of season, a downpour every afternoon. "White rain," they called it. You could drown in it. Then it stopped and the dust returned. She and Feli moved out of the hotel to an old apartment house in El Peñon, a long narrow chain of rooms one opening into another, without a corridor. It had no closets or refrigerator, but they liked the wealth of empty rooms and it was cool and dark and close to the market place.

ONE morning in April, as the, storms hung like a blue veil over the mountains, she walked to the butcher shop in the Plaza Girardot to buy meat for the weekend.

There were several people ahead of her, but the butcher wiped his bloody hands and smiled at her. "I help you, Missus," he said in English.

"*Salchichas tiene?*" she asked, avoiding his fond eyes.

"No, there is no sausage, you must come on Monday for that."

"Then a loin. You have a beef loin?" She fumbled in her straw bag for her list while he stared at the front of her dress.

"I have good beef loin. I have it in the chiller six days as Missus Woodhouse of the Malaria Inspections likes it. She is *Americana* like you. I know how to please *Americanas*. She always buys here, Missus Woodhouse. The beef is tender to cut with a...spoon?"

"A fork," Dorie said.

Three dusty children came behind the counter, and crowded around him. The tallest of them, no higher than his thigh, held up a handful of coins.

"A quarter of beef rib, and hurry our Mama said."

He ignored the child, held up a loin and trimmed off the gristle. Dorie observed the meat blandly, not touching it, trying to convey her confidence in him, at least in this matter. A woman, who had come in behind her wearing tight-fitting mourning serge, reached across and imbedded her thumb in it. "You don't ever give me such a good piece," she commented. "Listen, I need a two-and-a-half pound chicken."

"My Mama said hurry," shouted the child. "And we also want three caramels."

The butcher gave her a despairing look, then shut himself

up in the freezer. The noon closing of the shops was imminent. He came out with a second loin. "Maybe you like this better."

"No, no, the first is fine."

"You choose. There is no hurry." He turned to attend to the chicken, selecting one from the freezer and dropping it on the scale. "Exactly two-and-a-half pounds." The woman in mourning black went behind the counter and the butcher looked at her legs.

"How much?" she asked.

"Fifty *pesos*," he answered warily.

"You give it to me for less...It cost me forty."

"That's a joke. Give me a smaller one, then." The butcher said nothing, and selected another.

"Why is it so red?" she asked, fingering the cellophane wrapper.

"The freezing does it."

"Haven't you any fresh ones?"

"No, madam."

The woman fanned the exposed tops of her breasts with her flat pocketbook, and fingered the chicken thoughtfully.

"How much is a hen?"

"Ten *pesos* a pound." He looked toward Dorie. "I'll be right with you, Missus."

He rounded up some bones from the table, swept them into the child's basket, and leaned over the counter to Dorie. "The *chinitos*, I don't mind. They're poor. They always buy bones, always bring the exact change. They don't care what color the meat is. I don't mind the brats. It's her kind..." He made a filthy gesture toward the women in black. "She thinks this here is the loaves and the fishes. One chicken costs me forty *pesos*. What can I do?"

• 55 •

"Where did you learn English?" she asked.

"In Trinidad. My father work for the sugarcane there. I speak good?"

"Yes, good."

"The frozen ones have no flavor," said the woman.

He stared at the woman's tight black dress, her dirty feet in plastic scuffs. *"Bueno.* I will give you a fresh one. I have one saved for a customer. I will give it to you, eh?"

"Let me see it," she said cautiously.

He put it on the table for her to inspect, and went to shoo the bitch with dangling teats out of the shop. Dorie pointed to the first beef loin. "I'll take this one."

"Very good. I clean it for you."

"And three caramels!" the child boomed, holding up a coin.

"Five *centavos* you give me, eh?" The butcher showed Dorie the coin, which had long ceased to have any value. "Five *centavos*. He thinks he is speculating on the market." He opened a cellophane pack of caramels, costing ten *centavos*, removed three for the child, and offered the coin to Dorie.

"You collect these?"

"Oh, yes, for a friend in New York." She put the coin, which would purchase three candies out of a pack of six, into her straw bag.

"Soon there won't be any left, like the old *centavo*. I haven't seen one of those since Berrios was president. Will it be anything else?"

"Not just now, thank you." She gave him a hundred *peso* bill. He put it absently in the register, then counted fourteen *pesos* into her hand. "In your country, they desire something, they pay the price. Here it is shameful. They pinch, they pinch and they do not buy…" Turning away from her he said, "Disgusting widow! *Viuda de mierda!*" under his breath.

The woman picked up the unfrozen chicken and with great delicacy sniffed under a wing.

Dorie fished in her straw bag.

"You can be sure it smells better than you do!" he screamed. "Look at that!" to Dorie "Look at that! You can be sure, you can be sure that bird smells better than she does!"

After a moment, the woman laughed and gave the butcher a look of sly complicity, then pushed the bird toward him across the counter.

"I'll take it."

"Ah, ah! Good! Good! Fifty *pesos. Fifty pesos* for a two-and-a-half pound chicken is cheap!" He slipped the chicken and Dorie's beef loin into wax paper cones, grinning like a man who has just had sex.

OPENING an exercise book on top of *El Nacional,* which lay folded in his lap, Ordóñez noted the usual. Haníbal and Don Amable Rosero sat at a table in the open-fronted café waiting for Tiburcio, who always went into his office for an hour after lunch on Saturday in order to distinguish himself from Amable Rosero and Haníbal, who had no offices. The table, at which these two had been sitting since noon, was littered with scribbled ledger sheets and empty bottles of Polar Beer.

Tiburcio disciplines himself, Ordóñez thought. The richest man in Conahotu, owner of mines, pasture lands, commercial and residential buildings, opens his law office six days a week. Ordóñez approved of this discipline. One would have to be raised like Haníbal to gloat over having nothing to do. Ha! There he was.

Emerging from the offices of Gómez, Franco, y Lara, the firm founded by two uncles of Lilia's, Tiburcio turned and locked behind him the great carved door recessed in the side of the courthouse. Then, with a mixture of solemnity and good spirits, he steered along Zacour Avenue toward the cafe. Tiburcio wore a white linen, suit with three buttons and carried a tooled leather briefcase of the type used by landowners in the province of Los Chorros. He shut himself up in his office for two hours, Ordóñez thought, now he comes to the cafe like a man deserving refreshment. Look how he steers his belly, as if it were an ark full of treasure, how he pauses to salute God as he passes the cathedral! As if God were one of his creditors. He is a prince, Don Tiburcio. Since El Cacique, there has been no one like Tiburcio Gómez.

Haníbal and the Ecuadorian, Amable Rosero, stood up at the sight of Tiburcio, and tossed their arms around his shoulders. Tiburcio gave each of them a small hug, keeping his right hand on Haníbal's forearm, while his left adjusted a pocket flap and fumbled at the back of a chair—these last being gestures in parentheses. Ordóñez regarded this ability to subordinate one action to another as the essence of a fine manner. There were men, like Vice-Consul Plimford, who pulled up their socks with too much emphasis. Tiburcio did have a fine manner.

The three sat down. Haníbal, left knee joined to right elbow, spoke and Tiburcio listened to him (at the same time, summoning a waiter with a parenthetical wave over his head, another gesture not all men could have managed). Ah, Tiburcio, what a prince you are! It is a fact that there are few men in this world in which greed is as gracefully posited as it is in Tiburcio Gómez.

And where, exactly, does his princeliness lie? I must

discover..."The sleeves," he wrote in his notebook: "The sleeves of Tiburcio's linen jacket bulge at the back, as if inflated..."

Could it be that he stretches them out of shape so often by having his arm lifted over someone's shoulder? A good fellow, Tiburcio. He takes an urgent interest in your health. If I were to go over to speak to him now, he would tell me I looked underfed and remind me of Lilia. Tiburcio was the most tender of all when she died. Ah, he remembered the women, all the women lying in *doña* Luz's bed, weeping—women take to bed for all their important acts. And the children with the wreaths, grinning, threatening mayhem, and Tiburcio, upright, brought order. "Here, drink this *doña* Constanza, and walk on Luz's arm...Here now, we must organize this differently..." Yes, Tiburcio possesses. That's what it is. His money and his family are extensions of him, like the mines he owns in the mountains...

A man is what he possesses. And what does Ordóñez possess? A half-built house on Cuarta Bis Street, his three *chinitos,* four hens who lay eggs only every other day...

"Hello, Mr. Ordóñez." Doña Constanza stood in front of him, holding a paper cone of raspberry shaved ice.

"How are you, my dear Warsaw?"

"I am fine. And you? You've found work, I hear."

"Yes."

"I was glad to hear it. I've been to the butcher's. We have an apartment, Feli and I..."

"Felicia Cantru, who went around with the sculptor Pepe Anzoa?"

"Yes, In El Peñon. We cook and shop." She sat down beside him on the bench . "Usually I enjoy it, the shopping," she said. "But today it's been unpleasant."

"Ah, so..."

She told him what had happened at the butcher shop.

He laughed. "It's true. We'd sooner trust the Horned One than each other! But why should it trouble you?"

"I feel it will harm me!" she cried.

"But how, how harm you? With you, he conducted himself properly."

"That's just it!"

"I don't understand." He shook his head slowly. "You must not give it such importance."

She struggled to explain her reaction, to herself as well as to him, staring away from him in her effort, across the plaza to the cafe which spilled out of the flank of the courthouse. "It's as upsetting to be praised for something you're not responsible for as to be blamed...

"Do you come here often?" she changed the subject.

"Almost every day."

"Why?"

"I observe."

"What do you mean?"

"I observe. Just this moment, I am observing that my wife's cousin Tiburcio's jackets bulge about the upper arms. Now, I am thinking there has to be a precise reason for this and that I must discover what it is. There are always reasons for things, my dear. Life always has reasons, precise as a razor's edge. I read in *El Nacional* this morning that a certain stone image carved by a Chibcha Indian a thousand years ago had been stolen from a museum and had turned up holding down a pile of newspapers on a sidewalk in Charagua. It was said to have been worth five hundred thousand dollars. Everything has its worth."

"I don't see..."

"Everything becomes, eventually, a product, you see. Everything has its value. My product is this mystery of Tiburcio's sleeves explained. What will they pay me for this? They are paying, presently, five hundred *pesos* for a cubic meter of gold ore. What will they pay me to explain this mystery…?"

"You wish to become rich, Mr. Ordóñez?"

He laughed. Tears came. "Ah, my dear Warsaw…"

I love this man, she thought. I love this man.

"My dear Warsaw…"

"West," she said. Dorie West."

"Yes…yes, Miss West, I know. You liked the poem…"

"Yes."

"Well, well, and you took yourself off the board that other morning."

"I had a very enjoyable evening."

He sat looking at her, nodding thoughtfully. "Perhaps we should try it again, eh? There cannot be a thief every night."

"Not there," she said.

"Not there…?" he repeated.

"Not at your house."

"Ah, yes, yes." He was silent.

"Of course, of course, you are right," he said "Somewhere else, then," he said. "Have you been to Tocayo?"

"No."

"Tocayo is the most beautiful piece of beach in the world," he said, "though only I know that. Yes, we shall go; we shall go to Tocayo."

"I would like that very much," she said.

ON their second day at Tocayo, Dorie said to Ordóñez. "Perhaps tomorrow will be a better day."

"Probably not. It's what we deserve, this rain."

"Why?" she asked.

He tapped the rock where he sat with a stick, causing a number of little crabs, the color of the rock, to scuttle into crevices. "It's what we get for celebrating other people's holidays," he said.

"How do you mean?"

"It's simple. Of course this holiday isn't at the proper season, because it isn't our revolution we're celebrating. We import our holidays along with Ford chasses and frozen green peas. How could we deserve any better?"

Labor Day in Ciudad Conahotu corresponded to Moscow's May First celebration. It fell on a Friday. Ordóñez had talked to a driver friend of his into driving his sister, children, and himself over the mountains to the beach at Tocayo.

Friday afternoon it rained. They sat on the cottage porch and played dominoes. In front of them sky dissolved into sea. Behind was a rim of glossy rain forest on which the raindrops smacked loudly between were their two arks: one for the children and the sister, the other for Dorie and Ordóñez. The other side of the sheet of water was a bamboo pavilion with a thatch of palm leaves, where meals were served. At five o'clock, since it was still raining, they put on bathing suits and went over. The Spaniard who ran the bar and gave them some rum to warm their stomachs. "The rains are a little early this year," he offered, "but there's no doubt it's the start of the season."

"Might not tomorrow be better?" asked Dorie.

"Unlikely."

• 62 •

A boy carrying a basket of oysters came in. Some large limes among the gray oysters gathered all the light left in the day.

"Look," she said. "Where do they come from?"

"Chivacoa," said Ordóñez. "They will be fresh. He got them this morning." He signaled to the boy, who brought over his basket and began opening oysters with his penknife and squeezing lime juice over them before handing them to Ordóñez.

"Do you come all the way from Chivacoa every day?" Dorie asked the boy. He frowned as if he found human speech disagreeable. Ordóñez offered her an oyster, but she refused. He finished them himself and paid two *pesos*. The boy bought rum with one of the *pesos*, put the other in a plastic bag in his pocket. He buried the empty shells in the sand and was on his way down the beach, the limes in his basket like little suns.

The Spaniard closed the bar temporarily and went back to the kitchen to fry the fish and chunks of *yucca* root and plantain. "There are some peppers in vinegar if you want," he said. "Bring everything you have," said Ordóñez, who had paid for the weekend in advance. Alicia cut the children's food up into small bits and picked the bones out of the fish. She didn't begin eating until the children had nearly finished.

Luis slid from his chair, and disappeared under the table Presently Rita and Lily complained about him. His father pulled him out. A chair was overturned. "Savage!" Ordóñez shook him. The boy ran outside. "I'm afraid," said Alicia. "The water."

"I'll get him," said Dorie.

She walked down the beach in the direction the boy had taken. The mist allowed only a few yards of clear vision. The sand was littered with sticks and shells. She picked up and discarded several shells, keeping a piece of coral to show the boy, to cheer him.

But she didn't find him. Ordóñez caught up with her, and she showed him the coral. "I don't see Luis. Will anything happen to him?"

"No. He is only hiding. Are you cold?"

"No. Let's walk a ways. Oh, here's a dark pink shell. I think I'll keep it."

"You can see Chivacoa from here on a clear day," she said. "Off there to the west."

"How long did it take that boy to walk from there?"

"All morning, perhaps. You have to go inland at Cata, because of the cliffs."

"Will he sell a lot of oysters?"

"Yes, on good days."

They reached the breakwater. "Look, there's Luis out there on the rocks," said Dorie. The boy's silhouette was discernible against the mist.

"It's getting dark, Luis. Go in," said his father.

The boy came off the rocks and walked away without looking at them.

They came to a platform at the edge of the water. "What is this?" she asked.

"They embark prisoners."

"What prisoners?"

"Political prisoners. To El Burro Island. You can't see it today. It's off there to the south."

"Are there many people out there?"

"No, only a few old men that El Cacique put there. The gentlemen in Charagua now send their enemies to The Model Prison."

She stood on the broken boards, in the rolling mist. "Is there a boat?"

"El Cacique kept a wooden barge. When it was not in official use, he and his officers had parties aboard. Now there's a motor launch, I suppose."

"It's awful, awful," she said. "What were their crimes?"

"They thought the wrong thoughts."

"Published them, you mean?"

"El Cacique didn't know how to read."

"But others could read to him."

"He had no need of that. He read men's minds."

"I can't believe that."

"He was called 'The Wizard.' Many times he would suddenly fix his eyes on one of the men around him and say, 'That one who plots against me.' Evidence would turn up supporting him."

"Manufactured evidence."

"No, no. His powers were quite real. They became legendary."

"And you, Paco," she said. "Feli told me…"

"El Cacique never feared me. Quite rightly."

"But you planned…you and the others, the journalists…"

"He died in his bed, I told you. He died in his bed."

They walked a little way down the beach and turned. "We might as well go back," he said.

"In a minute. I'm a little put off by that cottage."

"I'd forgotten the bunk beds they have here. And they're nailed to the floor. Damn!"

"We can put the mattresses on the floor in between. Paco…

"Yes?"

• 65 •

"I feel a terrible attraction to you."

"You must always discuss," he said.

"I suppose I must…"

"I am unaccustomed. You shame me."

"Why should I shame you?"

"I worry…"

"Why? Why?"

"It is a risk for you to take up with me. No good ever came of it…"

"My dear Mr. Ordóñez, do you remember that night at Plimford's, you handed me the little firecracker to throw…?"

"I remember."

"You said, 'Will you take a chance, *Señorita,* a charge that is in the right end of this object?'"

"Yes."

"Well, I have taken that chance," she said.

At one a. m. they woke.

"Damn!"

"What is it?" she cried.

"A bat. Turn on the light."

"I am afraid to. I'd rather not see. It's so damp. Have you slept?"

"Yes."

"I haven't much." He laid his hand on her breast. His love making had been a replay of the unbuttoning of the costume a month before joined now to its rough conclusion and sudden pulling out. She had no contraceptives. You couldn't buy them here and she had made no efforts to bring any with her. He was gentler this time, exploring her with his tongue in places where her previous lover had never gone. She recognized in him an exclusive lover of woman, not fastidious about odors, about higher and lower parts of her, approaching her the way a careful doctor might approach a body, and her body expanded slowly to this new revelation.

He fell asleep soon after. She lay awake beside him several hours, then moved her mattress to the upper bunk and slept.

The bat woke them again at three.

"How did it get in?"

"The screen is torn."

"They carry rabies. What horror!"

"I'll turn on the light."

"No. It's quiet now. Sleep."

She slept again, but lightly, hearing him move about. Finally she spoke.

"What are you doing now?"

"Reading this newspaper I found on the floor of the bathroom."

"But why?"

"I am awake."

"The bat?"

"It is not moving. I have the bathroom light on. Shall I try to get it out?"

"No, don't. It'll fly at us." She got up and put her nightgown back on. "That newspaper must be at least a year old…"

She started crying. He had converted her to a sensualist in one night. She couldn't bear his distancing himself into a newspaper. "Oh God!"

"What is it? God in heaven, what is it!"

"We have such bad luck!"

He laughed. "Ah, Warsaw…!"

• 67 •

"I'm crazy about you, Paco. You can do anything you want with me: hurt me, abandon me..."

"But I wouldn't do that. I'm not an evil man. I spill my seed on top of your belly, but if anything happens, I'll take care of you."

"Of me and Lily and Alicia and Rita..."

"Not a very large family."

"It is. And this weekend is costing you too much..."

"Be quiet. You shame me."

"I don't mean to shame you."

"Hush now and go to sleep. You are a good girl. Go to sleep."

OCTAVIO Ramos, the taxi driver, had a woman who lived in the village of Tocayito nearby. He spent the night at her house and, late in the morning, returned to the beach to drink the Spaniard's stock of rum.

"Ordóñez, *hombre!*" he greeted Ordóñez when he met him at eleven in the palm-thatched pavilion, "The *Americanita*, tell me, is she a dream?"

"Be quiet, Octavio. You have no soul, and I don't like to hear you talk."

"Drink, then."

"No."

"Come on. Your gut will mildew. It begins to rain, no? Here, drink just a taste to keep away the rot. I should think an education must improve a woman, no? My Clotilda asks me for money to repair the roof the minute I finish with her. Some delicacy must be an agreeable thing. Of course, the roof will have to be fixed. I promised to bring her a piece of zinc but I didn't think the rains would start so soon. What a barbarous day. It won't clear till tomorrow noon. What's the matter with you, man? Is it so serious? Yes, I see, an educated woman is serious."

At about five in the morning, Dorie had crawled into the upper bunk and slept until eleven-thirty. At noon, when she came out to the pavilion, the Spaniard gave her coffee and fish chowder. It was cloudy, but not raining yet. Ordóñez was out on the jetty with the children. Octavio Ramos had dragged the back seat of his taxi to the beach and was taking a nap on it. There was a small group of people having drinks in the bar. A number of cars had left the day before, but today the public beach was crowded.

Alicia came to the table and Dorie spoke to her resolutely. "It was a terrible night. There was a bat and neither of us could sleep."

Alicia had a way of picking up sentences and setting them down in the middle. "Yes, it must have…Rita woke up with a…We shall all…Where are the…?"

"Paco has them out on the jetty. Will you have some chowder with me? It's quite good."

"I don't see…Oh, yes…No, thank you, not just now. I will get the children. Octavio Ramos is in a stupor, I suppose. I was thinking we might as well go back, since it is not nice."

"Oh. I had decided to stay."

"Oh well, then, yes."

"No. If you want to go, we shall go. I'll talk to Paco."

She went out to the jetty. Ordóñez and Luis watched a boy fishing. Beside them on the rocks were three expiring porgies. "Alicia wants to go back. Rita has a cold."

"Impossible. Ramos has a woman in Tocayo. He won't take us today."

"Oh, dear. Well, I'll take care of the girls for a while.

Alicia is tired."

She took them walking up the beach to the public area, where they could buy coconut milk. The public beach occupied the northern half of the shallow bay known as Bahialagrande, and was separated from the Spaniard's establishment by a low wall of scrap lumber and palm debris. It was crowded with family parties, which had come in taxis and pickup trucks, bringing kitchen chairs and tables, mattresses, hammocks, pots, food, and their aged in parlor chairs. Yesterday's oyster boy—or perhaps it was another—was crouched beside his basket, passing opened shells for the fathers of the families. A coconut vendor lopped off the heads of two coconuts with his machete and handed them to Lily and Rita, who tipped back their heads prodigiously and sucked at the openings. Motherless little things.

"Shall we look for shells?" asked Dorie.

The two girls walked on a distance in silence. Then Rita said, "My teacher, Hermana Sardi, has a little vase with shells stuck all over it on her desk. Also she has a little pill case with shells stuck on the lid. She told me she's going to give the pill case to me. All the other girls are jealous."

"She must like you," said Dorie. Rita didn't answer, and kept looking straight ahead. She was a hard child, adult in manner.

"Hermana Sardi's sister-in-law had to have both her breasts cut off and then she died. Hermana Sardi says that never happens to nuns. Alicia says I will be a nun."

"We could make a box with shells on it," said Dorie. "If you could find enough shells."

"It wouldn't be the kind they sell in the *Almacen del Clero*."

It began to rain lightly. The many palm thatch kiosks

that lined the beach were all occupied by families. The kiosks leaked badly. A more substantial one offered snacks for sale. They went in, and bought some guava squares. "I feel sorry for all these people in the rain," said Dorie.

"I don't," said Rita. "I feel sorry for Serafina." Serafina was her cat, left at home.

Behind the counter, a baby slept in a hammock, and a woman cooked on a kerosene burner. "May we have some coffee?" Dorie asked the young girl who had sold them the guava paste. She served them three cups, without saying a word. The baby began to cry and Lily went in and moved the hammock to and fro. The coffee was very hot. Dorie left hers on the counter to cool, and stirred some grayish sugar into Lily's cup. In a corner were some boxes, which the young girl told them they could use to sit on. Another child came from behind the counter-partition, where she stood drinking a brown liquid from a nursing bottle. The floor of the kiosk was made of waterlogged planks. Dorie thought of nights—couplings, writhings, births—in that back room. Her breasts ached.

"There's Papa!" shouted Lily.

"What are you doing here?" Ordóñez said to Dorie in English.

"Waiting for the rain to stop."

"It won't stop. Come out of there!"

After supper they drove into the town of Tocayo for drinks at a little cement block, zinc-roofed hotel, run by Germans. The plastered interior was ingeniously painted to resemble wood paneling. Such pains, thought Dorie, to produce so ill an effect. Some Black Forest curio factory had produced the rest of the decor. It was cozy, however, and worked on their deprivation.

• 71 •

"It would cost us three hundred *pesos* more to have a bed here," he said.

"I have that, and a little more. Come on now. We're both suffering."

"No. It would make me ashamed."

"All right. We'll have another *triple sec* then?"

"It's bad stuff. They make it out of sugar alcohol." He ordered them rum and a plate of sliced limes. "You are a good girl," he said.

"Am I?"

"I cannot degrade you."

"Why should you?"

"I have that wish somehow. I must…"

"To degrade me?"

"Yes."

"I understand. It's what women wish for, do you think?"

"Perhaps. But women like you cannot be degraded. You are, as Octavio Ramos says, an educated woman and everything that happens to you with me, you have imagined in advance…"

"Go on."

"You take away a man's power to hurt you."

"I see. I imagined this hotel beforehand, this lamp with a pink shade that has *Mein Liebhaber* written on its base, all these obscene shellacked plaques and barometers and heart-shaped chairs."

"Yes."

She laughed.

"That proves it. You laugh in recognition."

"Paco, can't we get a room?"

"Give me the money."

She gave him a five hundred *peso* bill. He went to the desk, signed a book with their separate names, and followed her down a hall with a red carpet and red velvet wall hangings. Educated woman.

"Let me just warn you," Feli said. "You go through a period when everything here just *charms* you. I know. It happened to me, you know, with Pepe. I mean, Pepe was just part of the picture, and it was so charming…discussions in cafes and all that. But when Pepe went sour, all the rest of it went sour too. And another thing, you get to thinking you can change them, save them…well, forget that."

"I don't think I would do that," Dorie said.

"Well, wait and see. You may come to it. There comes a feeling of…of futility. and you want to get out, you just want to get out."

"I don't think," said Dorie, "that we should allow ourselves to be deterred, by…others' disillusionments, from experiencing whatever…"

"Well, no."

"But I'll remember what you've said."

"If you could know how much I want to leave! It's either that or meet some wealthy industrialist and move out to La Cecilia!"

"I don't believe you mean that."

Feli laughed. Her gamin face was slightly blotchy from too many years of strong sun, and she kept it coated with white powder. "I absolutely mean it."

"What would you do in La Cecilia with all those doctors' wives and card players?"

"If you spend enough time in Ordóñez's bedroom, you'll know what I mean."

• 73 •

"How do you know what Paco's bedroom looks like?" Dorie asked.

"Oh, I know, I know!"

"Listen, Feli, it isn't some romantic notion of squalor. It isn't!"

"What is it, then?" They were eating *ceviche* in the evening breeze on their bit of neglected patio.

"You said about Pepe," Dorie began, "that he was part of the picture, a man in a setting…"

"Yes."

"I think that's what it is… Feli, did you ever know anyone before who loved his country…?"

Feli laughed.

"Yes, yes, it's funny. None of us can carry it off, not gracefully…not gracefully as he does. It's his gift."

Feli stood picking the dead branches off the ragged *papaya* tree which wouldn't bear fruit because there was no male tree inside the wall. "It's a country that could stand some loving, I guess," she said. "But what good does it do, Dorie, what good?"

RICAURTE paid a call at Ordóñez's house, and found that he was out. He decided to wait. Establishing himself in one of the leatherette chairs, he asked Rita to bring him coffee and, upon being served, asked her to tell him the product of nine times seven.

"I don't know the nine table yet," she said.

"You know the sevens," Ricaurte said. "Think."

She sat sullenly in the windowsill, staring out at the street through the grating.

"Children nowadays don't think," Ricaurte said. "That's the trouble with them."

She continued staring out the window. "There's Poppa, there's Poppa," she cried.

Ordóñez came in. "Ho, man, I'm sorry, I must go out again. I am to be godfather to my cousin's last *chinito*. She has nine. I am her last resort. I must get ready." He went to a spigot in the patio and began to lather his face. "Tell me, man, why you're here," he called down the corridor, "I am listening." He carried a basin of soapy water to a mirror hung above the sewing machine and shaved himself hurriedly.

"I have done you a favor," Ricaurte said. "I have made a proposal to Mr. Hillyer."

"Is that so."

"I said to him, 'Suppose you were to forgive Ordóñez? He will work; he will work like a mule,' I told him. I reminded him that you have advantages, that you are a man of culture, that you have traveled, that you speak English. Listen, they need a teacher. There is sickness."

"I know."

"'Ordóñez and I, we do not get sick,' I told him. 'We resist these tropical bugs.'"

"I have spoken to him also."

"What?"

Ordóñez took a tie that was hanging over a picture frame and knotted it around his neck. "I have spoken to Mr. Hillyer, myself."

"Is that so?"

"I went to see him."

"Ha! And...?"

"We had an interesting conversation. He told me a long story about a man he knows at Cartones-Fiberboard who is experimenting with native fibers, with the use of the residue of the sugar cane, the *bagazo,* to replace a portion of the raw material that is presently imported."

"Yes, yes…"

"Whereupon he offered Miss Vitale's class to me. Miss Vitale has a persistent biliousness and is frustrated in her pursuit of marriage to an indigent resident doctor at the University Hospital…so she is taking her sorrows back to where-ever-it-is, in the state of Missouri."

"Ah, ha!" said Ricaurte.

"You see his reasoning?"

"Yes, yes, the native fiber…"

"He is a complex man, Mister Hillyer. There is in him a social scientist who theorizes that, well, with these people it is a matter of mis-education, that they are damned by late-weaning, degenerate Catholicism, rote learning. Then there is, inside the social scientist, a more trustworthy being who says: 'They are damned, so they are damned. Let them punish themselves, though I should like to be the one who gives the lashes.'"

"Ah, yes," Ricaurte said, "You are not entirely the fool I thought. So you accepted his offer?"

"Yes, yes. For I began thinking: this social scientist wishes to have his experiment with his native fibers, let him have it. For I have my experiment, too…"

"What is that?"

"Never mind that, Ricaurte."

"Alcibiades is not going to continue to write in the *Prensa Libre*, I sincerely hope."

"No, no Alcibiades has undergone a transformation," Ordóñez said.

"Oh, well. As I said, you are not as great a fool as I thought." Ricaurte stood up to leave. "You have no doubt noticed that it is preferable to be better underpaid than not paid."

"I don't agree with your line of thinking, Ricaurte."

"To the devil with all that. Listen, just one thing: don't let any association of yours with the Pisanista Party be found out."

"Pisano," said Ordóñez, "Our Pisano won thirty percent of the vote in the last election. If he comes to power, we shall have to pack up our little school and take it elsewhere."

"When Pisano comes to power, the army will allow him two months to play his little games. Goodbye, then, man," said Ricaurte, and he left.

She came upon him cranking the duplicating machine and was suddenly alarmed. "My dear!"

He stopped the whirling drum. "What is it?"

She breathed a laugh. The letter had come into her mind: the seditious letter printed on this machine. "What are you printing?"

He showed her a science manual. Wild *Mimosa Pudica*, esoteric native herb, of the family of the acacia…

FROM his bench in the plaza, Ordóñez noted that Haníbal and the Ecuadorian, Amable Rosero, were busy filling a ledger with figures. "A pact with hopelessness, that was Don Amable's life," he noted in his notebook. "A chemist, graduated in Quito, Amable cannot obtain legal employment here without validating his degree, which would cost him five thousand *pesos* to line the pockets of the examiners. Thus he earns his *centavos* from the lugubrious materials he formulates in a laboratory on the rooftop of his house, working stark naked, putting on a dirty white coat if anyone calls. He is married to a schoolteacher. One may deduce what one wishes from that…"

"They are scheming, Amable and Haníbal. They have purchased a new ledger in which to compute what they will earn marketing Amable's latest alchemy. They believe they will become rich one day, with one of Amable's depressing inventions. Ha! If they were not atheists, you would think they were computing what was owed them in a later life...as if failure ever earned success..."

Tiburcio had not come from his office. He found it refreshing to turn his thoughts to Tiburcio. "The rich are a source of pleasure." he wrote in his notebook. "The grandeur of Tiburcio's house enriches the community. In fact, one might say that a city is beautiful in direct relation to the number of rich men it possesses..."

Lilia, he recalled, could read with pleasure of a starlet's fur-lined bath reported in *Romances de Hoy*. Lilia had been a saint. She was too simple for envy. He entered these thoughts in his notebooks also, for lack of anything better. He felt conscious of a vague dissatisfaction. What was it?

This situation with the American girl is wrong. It makes me envious, yes.

If I had a car like Tiburcio.

If I could afford to have a discreet servant in the house, instead of my sister...

If I could even afford a washing woman with the buttons sewn on the front of her dress!

A bad situation.

What do I want? What do I want? Let me look frankly at my desires. That is the rational way prescribed by Dr. Voronoff.

Appalling.

I want no less than a beautiful and silent new wife, with Lilia's body. If I had money...if I had money, I would search this whole land and when I found such a woman, I would purchase her. Ha!

And the *Americanita?* Let us be honest now.

The *Americanita,* I would have for my devoted mistress, mind-mate, soul-mate…secure somewhere in an attractive little house, editing my books, translating them…

Appalling!

Let us suppose that it is true that all men fall into one of two types, the Amables and the Tiburcios. Ordóñez, then, must be assigned as an Amable. His notebooks and Amable's experiments are identical…

But could one choose? Could one chose to be a Tiburcio?

Yes, yes, this requires concentration. To be a Tiburcio, to ingest him as one ingests the Host, his body and blood. To possess, to possess his possessing, Yes!

But how to deflect Tiburcio from his daily round, as he steers his protuberant belly from the office to the cafe like an ark full of treasure…?

One must have something he wants. Something of value. What does Ordóñez have of value? A half-built house on Cuarta Bis Street, a chicken that lays an egg every other day, a pile of notebooks containing…

Hah! hah ha! The notebooks. Yes! yes yes yes!

"*Hola.*" Roberto Pino moved Ordóñez's notebooks to the end of the bench and sat down. Ordóñez had not seen Roberto Pino in three years. He had heard that he was in prison.

"So they've set you free."

"I wasn't in prison. The past three years I was living in La Victoria, letting the incident cool off. Now I am at my sister-in-law's on Second Street."

"And are you back in business?"

"Yes. Will I get an article from you? We publish in March. Two issues a month."

"I think I am not a political man anymore, discover I don't care anymore if there are fascists in the Christian Brothers."

"I don't believe it," said Roberto Pino.

"It is true."

"Then write something else. Anything. Controversy is what we're after."

"Listen, Roberto. One insults our honored president and is sent to the Model Prison for two months. One is treated well, and then invited to go to Spain for a rest. Is that what you want?"

"One takes whatever reprisal is the fashion. I don't concern myself with that."

"I tell you, Robert, I don't care about the present gentlemen in Charagua. El Cacique died in his bed, he died in his bed!"

"That is past."

"Yes. Yet one wants to risk a reprisal that is, well, that is a reprisal…A shot in the back…a shot in the back is like an embrace."

"You are crazy, Ordóñez."

"No, no. It is just that my thoughts are on something else. Listen, Roberto, suppose you had money. Suppose you had the money of Don Bernardo Mesa of the Tobacco Company, for example. Then you would no longer be an editor of a low circulation magazine, which must close down every few years, who signs himself 'Hippias Major.'"

"How so?"

"Well, now, let us consider. At the point where the irritability of 'Hippias Major' intersects the neediness of 'Hippias Major, there Roberto Pino exists. In the same manner, at the point where Ordóñez's notebooks intersect with his neediness, intersect with the fact that he is a schoolteacher, there Ordóñez exists. Right? Now...now we introduce a new factor: money, say, the money of Don Bernardo Mesa, let us say..."

"I don't follow you, *hombre*. It is a matter of redistributing wealth..."

"Redistributing wealth may be no easier than redistributing atoms. One does not know. One wishes to perform experiments."

"What experiments?"

"Ha! Let us say a diet rich in vitamins. Don Bernardo, it's said, has just fathered a son at the age of sixty-five."

"*Ay, hombre!*"

"Then it is said that malnutrition after a certain age is irreversible...Look, I got out of bed early yesterday morning to write in my book: 'Ordóñez is a schoolteacher out of necessity.' Necessity as philosophers use the term. 'What one is,' I wrote, 'is a cipher in one's cells. 'I was impelled by a peculiar urgency to write it down. One often feels this urgency waking out of deep sleep at an unusual hour. The mood passes, and I tell myself, after the day has begun and I sit with Alicia drinking coffee, that perhaps there is more value in an experiment, that that is the modern way. Suppose, just suppose, that Hippias Major were to possess the money now belonging to Don Bernardo of the Tobacco Company...?"

"As I said, it is a problem of redistribution..."

"Ah, man, I am sick of political indignation. For years I fed on it. I want some other food! One does not want the redistribution of wealth. One wants to say to Bernardo Mesa:

• 81 •

'Give me what is yours.' Simply that: Give me what is yours. So that one might know..."

"That is my experiment, Roberto. We shall no longer have hypotheses, eh. We shall know. We shall know! Introduce Hippias Major to money, eh? Introduce Hippias Major to money and we shall see what he will do, what desires he will fulfill."

"Ah, Ordóñez."

He laughed. "You are a good man, Robert. Who but you would print my ravings? I am glad to see you. I didn't think I would see you again."

"We are in the hands of gentlemen, as I said. There is talk of allowing Lisandro Reyes to come back and giving him a trial. It's the fair thing, they are saying. All are equal under the law, they say about Lisandro Reyes who stole our entire cattle industry!"

"What rubbish!"

"Yes! So *hombre*, you are nostalgic for the firing squad. All this fairness bothers you, eh? What are you doing at present?"

"I am teaching at the *Americanos'* school."

"Ah to what end?"

"To what end, man? To the end of eating!"

"Ah...I thought, I thought perhaps it was one of your... your experiments."

"Perhaps it is, perhaps it is, man."

"Ah, well. I am glad you are eating well..."

"There is divine madness, Robert, and there is simple madness. You understand? The second is common like dust, part of the chaos, atoms broken down to be reconstituted, like your redistribution of wealth. What relief it is for some men to die, Robert, to be reconstituted. We are slaves now.

When chaos is reconstituted, we could be masters...Is it possible? We each hold our life like a clay pot. We can drop it if we wish."

"You worry me, Paco. I ask you for an article, and what is this you are giving me...?"

"Ha! Yes! Listen, Robert, I will give you something, you hear. Where will I find you?"

"My sister-in-law's. Second Street. Across from the laundry. Number forty-seven. We will have a meeting the day after tomorrow. Will you come?"

"No. I am busy."

"Busy? What is your business?"

"The experiment. I am telling you. It is not just talk. I am planning to act. I am planning an action..."

"Ah! You are planning to lay hands on Don Bernardo Mesa..."

"Not Don Bernardo."

"Who then?"

"I cannot tell you now. I must not speak of it. Speaking drains energy."

"When will I see you then?"

"You will see me when you see me."

Roberto Pino gripped his shoulder. "Take care, *hombre*. You will get a fever of the brain. One does not act against one's nature without reprisals, remember that."

Tiburcio still had not come. It threatened to rain. It was likely Tiburcio had gone straight home in a taxi. Ordóñez packed up his notebooks and crossed the street to the cafe. Amable and Haníbal were conversing with Amable's brother-in-law, the priest.

"...the Pope has taken sex away from the poor devils. Not one of them can rise above it," Amable was saying.

"Father Lope at San Mateo published a paper on the diaphragm device, did you know?" Hanibal said.

"Of course, he gets his little titillation that way," said the priest. "What a country! Everyone out to get his little titillation. 'Only give us Father Lope's diaphragm device,' say my parishioners, 'and we'll be clean, industrious, everything we ought to be, just like the *Norteamericanos!*' A bright day dawning! All because of Father Lope's diaphragm device."

"Did you know they sell the Pill here, only the women don't know it? They have only to claim menstrual irregularity and they can get it. Yet they continue to douche with aspirin water and to jump up and down on the bed after…and to bear a child every year. Such ignorance is depressing."

Ordóñez sneezed. He had brought a cold from Tocayo.

"You ought to purge yourself," said Amable, "And take a garlic broth. I'll order you a Lux-Cola." Lux-Cola was a commercial blend of sugar, red dye, and carbonated water to which Amable attributed medicinal properties. Ordóñez usually protested; today he acquiesced. "Where's Tiburcio?" he asked.

"It's going to rain," Haníbal said. "He probably took a taxi home. You never come around anymore. You need to see Tiburcio?"

"Yes."

"What's the plot?"

THE following afternoon was sunny; the evening's storm was still a purple gathering on the mountain tops. Tiburcio resumed his routine. Ordóñez crossed the Calle Ochoa and detained his kinsman in front of the courthouse.

"Will you come across to the plaza with me for a moment?"

"I was just going to the cafe. Come with me."

"No, the plaza. I would rather, just for a few moments."

"All right," Tiburcio said, and took Ordóñez's arm. When they were out of sight of Amable and Haníbal, Ordóñez stopped to light the first cigarette he had smoked in eight years, then turned and faced his wife's cousin.

"Listen, Tiburcio, I am going to tell you something that is going to sound strange, very strange, to you. But it is all true, and I must tell it to you. It is important, to both of us..."

"Aah haah," said Tiburcio, planting his feet and crossing his arms. Tiburcio didn't smoke. He had smoked from the age of twelve to the age of thirty-seven. Then he had abruptly come to believe it was harming him and given it up. Likewise, he had given up keeping fighting cocks, after a dispute and the loss of a five hundred *peso* bet. Tiburcio never did anything that was harmful to him, or to his properties.

"It is this," said Ordóñez. "It is this: I have eyes, Tiburcio. I see many things. I see many things and I write them in my research. It is my vice. All of this you know..."

"I didn't know..."

"I have observed you, Tiburcio, for many years. It is all in my notebooks. And now the fruit is ripe."

"You are an odd one, Paco."

"You, Tiburcio, are a smart one. You outsmart the farmers, and get the mineral rights for the gold under their fields. You steal from them because they forget to put a twenty *peso* government stamp on the deeds to their lands. This I know. I know many things. You have a little girl staying over at Mama Plaschek's. She adores you I know that, too..."

Tiburcio jingled change in his pockets, and looked impatient. "You want to be a writer, my cousin? Maybe I know someone who can…"

"Shut up, Tiburcio. Don't get all warm and smothering. I know you, I tell you, I know you. The fruit is ripe…"

Tiburcio adopted an easy stance, looking him in the face as Ordóñez continued.

"Listen now, Tiburcio. You buy a piece of land with the idea that some day you will get back a high price for it. Is it not so?" Tiburcio made no motion. "It is so, then. You would not throw away the title to a piece of property…you will not throw away a title out of any…delicacy of feeling. Just so, just so. My research offends, I cannot simply throw it away. The public wishes to consume strips of raw human flesh. I am not responsible for the public's tastes."

Tiburcio stood staring across the plaza. The East was dark blue with a new storm.

"The public is ravenous to read that Ramón Márquez drives a sports model Mercedes, that he left a woman and baby in Barrio Meléndez to marry Lolita Peralta Why should the public not have you, Tiburcio, when you are a more important man than Ramón Marquez? Of course, it is fiction I write, but as I said, the public taste runs to raw human meat. They will know. They will know though that is not my purpose. None of this I am speaking of is my purpose. I have, if you can understand this, Tiburcio, a high purpose…A high purpose. Hah! Ah, Tibucio, do you think I am low? If I could be as low as you, then I would respect myself. So, let us speak simply: You are a man of great reputation and I will ruin you in the interests of my research."

"Where will you ruin me, Ordóñez? In *Romances de Hoy*? I am not a singer of ballads…"

"In Roberto Pino's periodical."

"Roberto Pino is in jail."

"Not so. I spoke to him yesterday."

"Ah well." Tiburcio looked away. He was smiling with his lips closed, blowing gently and repeatedly through his nose, like a horse. His right hand was in the pocket of his linen jacket. A woman offered a tray of turtles for sale. Ordóñez waved a hand to dismiss her. "It is very elementary," he said. "We will not go into my purposes, as I say. I tell you I cannot abandon my research without some recompense. You can understand that, Tiburcio. You are familiar with this kind of business. Let us be frank: I'm not at ease in these matters. I don't have your fine manner. Look, my hands tremble. My throat is dry. Hah! If you give me something, Tiburcio, I will not harm you."

Tiburcio blew his breath loudly through his nose, and Ordóñez continued before he could speak. "Yes, yes, I see, you are going to make this difficult. But I am decided, you see. My hands tremble, but I am firm..." The woman continued to offer her tray of turtle's. Ordóñez steered Tiburcio back toward the courthouse. The woman followed them at a distance. "We all have our little businesses, you see," he said, indicating the woman. "It is not surprising, then, that I should want to sell you something—be it your reputation, be it whatever..."

Tiburcio shifted his briefcase from his left hand to his right and moved toward the street. "I will speak to you," he said. "I will speak to you in a day or two." He stepped off the curb.

"Yes, *hombre*, yes."

Tiburcio crossed the street. Ordóñez watched to see if he would enter the cafe, where Amable and Hanibal still sat behind a table full of glasses and cups. He didn't. He crossed to the other corner and caught a taxi.

A WEEK passed. There was no word from Tiburcio.

"If he gives me something worth my while—a farm, a monthly check," Ordóñez thought, "I will become benevolent and tender like him. And I will write my books slowly and with no worries about publishing...

"But there will he no Tiburcio in them," he said out loud, and closed the notebook he had just opened. The fascination of the discarded alternative. Tiburcio had been his best subject.

"I love Tiburcio. My offense against him is unbearable to me at this moment. My skin prickles when I remember my words..."

He packed up his notebooks and crossed to the cafe. Haníbal and Amable were not there. They had gone to Charagua to buy flasks. Haníbal's brother-in-law, Father Lope, sat alone at a table. Ordóñez sat down with him.

"Notre Dame University, where is that?" the priest asked him.

"I don't know."

"When I was studying in Pileta, I won a scholarship there. My Superior didn't allow me to take it, so I came here. How is your cold?"

"Worse."

"I'll sign a dispensary certificate for you, if you want. The *Acción Católica* sends me a truckload of drugs every week. I spend all my time doling out prescriptions. Doctors overdo prescriptions for the poor. Saves them the trouble of a radical cure. Do you have a fever?"

"Slightly."

"Come, then. We'll walk over and get a bottle of Seperol." The priest paid his bill and they descended Magdelena Street, walking in the gutter because of the broken sidewalk.

"In Pileta, I studied English," said the priest.

"Pileta, in your dark canyon..."

"Barbara wrote that. He studied a year at the seminary. In the hotel in Pileta, there was no plumbing. Men put on masks to go outside to the patio to urinate. The masks hung in a row in the dining room. That's good, isn't it? You can't hide your acts of nature from the world, so you hide your face...

"I read *A Tale of Two Cities* in Pileta, in a simplified version. A young North American gave it to me, a convert..."

All this, thought Ordóñez, was the priest's way of telling him he knew about the *Americanita*.

"This young North American set an exaggerated value on his soul. All converts do. I gave him instruction for a year, and when he took his first communion, he gave a floor of paving stones to the church. A price on their heads was like a Pentecostal flame. They enter through a special door...A special door. It took him a long time to decide. The rest of us are brought in our mothers' arms, before the age of reason, yelp for five minutes in front of the baptismal font, and it's done. Seven years later the Bishop signs a certificate for us..."

They went through a screen door into the priest's study, which fronted right on Magdalena Street with barely a yard between door and street. An armoire stood open, exposing a row of lacy cassocks. "Seperol," the priest reminded himself. "Sit in that chair." He indicated a large leatherette armchair. "The others are broken."

Ordóñez sat. The priest fiddled at his desk, repeating the word "Seperol" as he fingered through a pile of record books. "You shouldn't take too much Seperol. It makes you sleepy and swells the eyelids.

"No such price on our heads," he murmured. "Woman

lost her third child this morning. 'You have enough other children, Hortensia,' I said. 'Console yourself with them...'"

Ordóñez was not listening. I love Tiburcio, he was thinking.

"Here is better than Pileta," the priest said. "If it weren't for this tin roof. This study is an inferno."

"It is hot," admitted Ordóñez. The priest ought to interest me, he thought. I ought to dedicate a notebook to him. Who was it who trailed after his compatriots with a notebook? Balzac? Gorki. Gorki cut down a tree every day after lunch, in the interest of self discipline. Discipline, discipline is everything. Every day like the one before. Damn. Damn Tiburcio. I cannot work with this matter still pending.

"Rosalia will bring coffee," said the priest.

"Never mind," he said. "And don't bother with the certificate."

"It's done. There." The priest finished noting the request in the record book. "My dispensary is just back here in the garage. The Renaults have no home anymore since *Acción Católica*, with its free drugs..."

"I'll feel better tomorrow."

"It's no trouble. Stay." The priest picked up the cat, which was rubbing against his ankles. "Look at Michica. She had an adventure yesterday. She went to live with the Italians at the butcher shop, but the prodigal has returned. I'll get your script. You sit there. I'll be right back. There's a *Life en Español* you can look at. It has pictures of spring in Alaska. I used to get it in English. Now you can't. The pictures are just as good. Stay there now." He went out.

The thought recurred.

I love Tiburcio.

He thought of people he had loved: his mother, his aunts,

the women in his family. He had loved the family women. The *Americanita* was too unlike them. Yet she loved him. He had never asked himself if Lilia loved him.

I love Tiburcio...

Was he caught off guard by my threat? A man like Tiburcio has had his reputation threatened on many occasions and not always by simple farmers he's cheated of their land rights.

The priest had not returned. He left without waiting.

FELI took her to the Zoological Garden to see El Cacique's caged animals.

It was dark and moist under the large silk cotton trees, and the buildings—the aviary, the aquarium built in the style of Mussolini's Rome—were charted with black lichens and mold. Already, at four o'clock, they were in the shadow of the mountains, which rose just here where the Road to the Sea flung itself up and over through rain forest to the beach at Catire. "It was beautiful once," Feli said. "He spent huge sums to have the animals shipped here. Now it's all run-down."

"I see."

"No one cares for the animals. The beggar boys feed cigarette butts to the elephant, and the monkeys are so bored they snatch you." Crocodiles and a hippo lay in a bog behind the aviary. "That old fellow," Feli pointed him out, "would come out of the water for the Old Man. No one else could get him to do it."

They ordered *badea* juice at the large kiosk with a tiled floor in the garden that had once belonged to one of El Cacique's daughters.

Dorie was silent. She felt so depressed: the gloom, the neglected animals.

"Ordóñez's room, eh?" Feli commented, seeing her state.

"No, no. It's him. He tells me nothing."

Feli took up the burden of talk. "When I was with Pepe, we lived in three little rooms in the Barrio Terrón. We had a bed, a cot for his kid, three steamer trunks, a table and a couple of stools. I had a poncho I put over one of the trunks and one day I bought three black cups in the market and put them on the trunk with the poncho and they looked so nice I thought I'd invite friends over for coffee. Well, Pepe saw my cups and right off moved his studio out of where it was in the bedroom, and took my corner. It was cooler, he said, and the light was better. He had to have it. So I moved my coffee cups out to the patio and had my friends in, and then there was an explosion. 'We can't have this,' he said. 'Either I have my work in this house, or you have your tea parties! We can't have both.'"

Dorie was frowning.

Feli laughed. "I'm basically a silly person," she said. "Pepe saw that..."

"Yes, it's true. What do I want? I want to go to Switzerland and have my ears pinned and my nose shortened. No, to really fight him, I would have to have been as sure of myself as he was. He knew absolutely what he wanted. I don't mean the socialism, I mean the work. When he couldn't work, he got nervous. He attacked people, he moved his studio, he took up the socialism. But it was the work that mattered. With Paco it is the socialism, isn't it?"

"I don't know...I don't know. It seems lately that it's something else. He talks of plots, of money, of what he'd do if he had money. Things aren't right. We never have peace. His sister is there, or there is a thief on the roof..." She sighed, then clapped a hand over her mouth. "Oh!"

"What is it?"

"My tooth aches. I lost a filling."

"Idiot! See a dentist."

They walked on the Avenida del Rio as far as the Plaza Girardot. Feli pointed out a dental clinic on the floor above a dress shop. "Monday you get an appointment, hear!"

Dorie nodded. "Yes, yes." They crossed to the Boulevard, and she purchased a piece of wool cloth from an Indian sitting on the steps of the Bank of Montreal. It pleased her. Woven into the center was the figure of a man standing beside a tree. The man was taller than the tree.

Monday, Dorie got off the school bus at the Plaza Girardot to see a dentist. Remedies are easily found if you keep your mind on them.

"I have twinges here, in this incisor, or maybe the tooth behind…if the doctor could see me now…"

"Doctor is at a conference. He'll be back next month." The receptionist was not aware of Dorie's intense concentration.

"Next month! When next month?"

"The fifteenth. Should I note you down?"

"Oh, no. Forget it. I'll let you know."

There were no other dentists in the plaza. She walked the six blocks to Ordóñez's house. Alicia was in Charagua visiting another sister. Dorie fed the chickens, gave Lily and Rita coffee and hot milk, then set out a place for Luis, who came later. After that she dusted the four leatherette chairs in the parlor and sat down on one of them to grade her workbooks. Only then did it occur to her that it was her birthday. Practically the whole day had gone by, and she hadn't remembered.

ORDÓÑEZ came in at six. She served him soup. "I'm twenty-five today. The whole day has gone by, and I've only just remembered."

"Has anyone been here?" he asked.

"No. Who are you expecting?"

"No one."

"Well, you seem to be expecting someone."

"I can't tell you."

"Why not?"

"Unlucky. Be quiet about it."

"You're expecting a bit of luck?"

"No, no, no luck. There is no luck for me. The law of averages is not even operative."

"Don't be silly…"

"What happens to one is a cipher in one's cells. That is my theory. I would do well to stick to it…you play a game, like *lulo*. It is a card game of pure luck. Ten times in fifty, Tiburcio will hold the ace of *oros*. Ordóñez will hold it five times, and Amable Campuzano, one. A cipher in the cells…"

The washing woman was on the patio beating the wet sheets on the cement floor. The parrot atop the refrigerator shrieked. "Big Beak," grumbled the woman. "Filthy old Big Beak."

"I don't understand what you are talking about," she said.

"Never mind. Give me some tomato with the soup. Damn him, though. I frightened him. I must have…"

"Who? Who have you frightened?"

"No one. Is this all the milk?"

"Luis had two cups. You've quit your job…"

"No, not that."

"What, then?"

I will not babble like Haníbal, he thought. Dorie thought he looked ill, hectic.

Ricaurte came. Ordóñez was giving him English lessons. "Did you know, Mr. Ricaurte, I'm twenty-five today. I forgot it was my birthday," she told him.

"Ah well," he said, "Congratulations! We will celebrate. I invite you to the grill."

66

"I'D like to go," she said. "Will you come, Paco? You're in a funk. Come for an hour or two. Please."

Ricaurte took a long time buying a bottle of Lambrusco at wine seller's on the corner. Then they walked along Semrad Boulevard, which terminated at a plaza with an obelisk in the center. The air was wet from early afternoon storm, but clear. The bank of clouds hanging over the mountains had lifted and scattered off to the West.

They sat at a table by the river. Ricaurte went over to the window and brought back pastries and a tray with and three glasses. The river roared with flood waters. It had turned the same reddish color as the muddy paths of Terrón Colorado, the slum neighborhood which climbed the slope of the hill behind them.

The sun was going behind the western range. She watched for the exact moment when the green left the grass and trees but was cheated in her observation by the street lights coming on. Ricaurte struggled with the cork in the bottle of Lambrusco.

"Are you going back to the *Colegio* next year, Mr. Ricaurte?" Dorie asked. "Everyone but us, it seems, is busy carving out a new career."

"What else would I do, Miss Dorie?"

She smiled. "True."

• 95 •

"If I win the lottery, then I will quit," he said.

"Do you expect to?" she asked.

"Someday I may win," he said. "I have a system."

"A system is good," said Ordóñez.

"If you do what most people do," said Ricaurte, "that is to put a small amount—five *pesos*—on the whole number every week, then you never win. The odds against you are several hundred thousand to one. No one ever wins that way. So, in my system, you don't waste money on the whole number unless you can put together enough money to buy many tickets. In my system you play the terminals. You put a small payment on the last number every week. I win six times that way, between five and six hundred a month."

"You won't retire on that," said Ordóñez

"Precisely. But, of the five hundred, I put two hundred each month on the whole number. Someday I may win." He succeeded in getting the cork out and poured three glasses of wine. "Health and dollars," he toasted Dorie, lifting his glass to touch hers.

"Thank you."

"I would say, 'Health and *pesos*' but, as they say, that's a devaluated toast," Ricaurte continued, "Always, I have the hope of winning. Gambling is a divine thing. One lives in a state of great emotion."

"I can see that," said Dorie.

"Yet I am prudent. The worst thing is to risk more and more money. If I don't win the terminal enough times in a month, I don't play the whole number."

Dorie lifted her glass a second time. "Luck," she said to Ricaurte.

In the darkness, the river roared.

"If it rains much more, all of Terrón Colorado will be

down here," commented Ricaurte.

"Why do they build up there?" asked Dorie.

"The widow of Adelberto Marcos gave the hillside to the people who were living on the sidewalks after Luis Montalba's militia disbanded," said Ordóñez.

"And they invited their brothers and cousins," said Ricaurte. "To hell with the widow Marcos' charity! Any son of a laundress would rather see himself washed down the mountainside every April than live as he should, planting rice in the interior!"

"It was a disinterested act," said Ordóñez.

"What was?"

"The widow Marcos' gift."

"Define disinterested."

"Apropos of nothing. What do you expect of a Marcos? Forty years ago they sat in their pajamas all day, playing dominos in their front yard."

"Marvelous! Apropos of nothing! Five hundred sons of laundresses living on a slippery mountainside. My oldest sister has eleven children apropos of nothing. Another has nine."

"Are you the last son, Ricaurte?" Ordóñez asked.

"Yes."

"I thought so. The last son is always a Jesuit. I have made a study."

Ricaurte refilled the glasses. "It's what every son ought to wish for," he said, "to be the last."

"The last son is the parents' weariness," said Ordóñez.

"And why should we be such monkeys for breeding?" Ricaurte asked. "You tell me that."

"Lisandro Gil, in *El Nacional,* says we're filling a continent before the planners in Washington take it away from us."

"Filling it with sons of laundresses," said Ricaurte. "What good is that?"

"You have no faith in the unrealized, Ricaurte. What is necessary is to sit under one of our trees and become aware of what is to be born of this soil, of this seed that is our race."

"That is lovely," said Ricaurte, "But I never think of such things. I think of my two hundred *pesos* that I win on the terminals, that someday will win me a million *pesos*. The wine is finished. What will you have?"

"A beer," said Ordóñez.

Ricaurte took the tray and crossed the little plaza to the grill opposite.

Dorie asked, "Why do you call Ricaurte a Jesuit? I don't understand."

"Sublimation," he said. "Ricaurte likes little boys. As far as I know he's never touched one."

"I still don't see."

"Sublimation is the difference between an Indian grinding corn and a man plotting a course to Venus. Except the Jesuit mentality cuts the process short, condenses it. We have an institution of unmarried younger brothers living with married sisters. They are the parents' weariness. They do not marry. They are good to their nephews—a relationship once removed, like the Jesuit's to the world. For everything, we have an institution. It makes up to us for the boys we didn't touch, or otherwise."

Ricaurte returned with three Polars. "Thanks, man," said Ordóñez. "Your Lambrusco was fine, but we'll get farther on Polar Beer."

THE alarm clock in the bedroom, which they usually set for midnight, didn't go off until 5 a. m. Dorie had taken a nap in the afternoon, set the alarm for suppertime, and had forgotten to reset it. In bars of moonlight, she picked her clothes off the floor, hung Ordóñez's shirt over a chair, finished the glass of rum left on the bureau, and slowly put her clothes on. The street was more desolate at five than it usually was at twelve. There were still taxis, however, at the stand on the Plaza Girardot. It was a driver she didn't know. He wordlessly took her straight home. Twenty-five years and one day old. Her tooth ached.

SUNDAY, Ordóñez walked to the chapel on Magdalena Street to hear Father Lope preach. Along the broken pavement, stumbling over their long white dresses, came April's little brides of Christ. Their hems and their first communion bouquets were dusty before they even got to the church.

He had never attended Mass at this church before, and was impressed by Father Lope. He had never seen any priest put more grace into his obeisance to the Host. After the Elevation, the little brides walked forward, attended by aunts, godmothers. He thought of Inca princesses led to the sacrifice. The sermon topic was taken from *El Nacional's* Friday headline.

"Future U. S. Astronauts Greet Soviet Counterparts."

Spain sends us these dark-jowled priests from Pileta, to help us interpret the headlines for us.

Luis asked, "Why are we at this church?"

"The priest is a friend."

"When will I make my first communion?" asked Lily.

"When Alicia returns," he told her. I have only half my

heart for my children any more, he thought.

They went around to the priest's study. Father Lope put a hand on shoulder. "*Hombre,* so these are your *chinitos.* They are three beauties. Your woman was a Peralta, no?"

"Yes."

"A strain of beauty runs in the Peralta family. My cousin's children are Peraltas from Aguadas. How is your cold?"

"Better."

"I have your *Seperol* on my desk. You took off the other day."

"No, no. None of your *Seperol.*"

"We'll walk up to the plaza then Father Clodimiro takes the next Mass."

Amable and Haníbal were at the cafe. Amable told Ordóñez he looked as if he wasn't eating well, ordered him a Lux Cola, and advised him to get some *Agua de Boldo* and to make a paste of pomegranate seeds to restore his appetite. He and. Haníbal were calculating costs of producing an apparatus for hydro massage of the breasts that an acquaintance had seen in Paris.

"It can increase their size or decrease it," explained Amable.

Afterward, Ordóñez recorded the conversation in his notebook. It gave him no pleasure, however.

TUESDAY at the cafe, there was a note from Tiburcio. Haníbal handed it to him. They could talk Wednesday, at Tiburcio's home, at five o'clock.

In spite of all his forethought, it came as a shock.

He is capable of shooting me, he thought, I will borrow a gun.

No, I will not. Ordóñez the schoolteacher does not shoot people.

WEDNESDAY morning he was cooler, prepared for whatever would come. Odds on what Tiburcio might do could be more or less accurately calculated. He knew that when his wife's cousin was still studying at the Christian Brothers he had knifed a companion who disturbed him while he studied. Everyone knew about the incident. Tiburcio invalidated the deed by the farmer who once insulted him. Tiburcio's men had him driven off his land.

Tender, benevolent Tiburcio just because he was a bastard, he never felt his manner needed to betray the fact...

And here was he, having acted boldly and maliciously but once in his life—only once in his life! Damn! And ever since he had been behaving like a bastard!

The Miraflores bus dropped him off in front of the Swedish Consulate on Seventh Street, and he walked up the hill to Tiburcio's house. Tiburcio lived among mercantile Jews and Lebanese, as well as North Americans who paid scalper's rents for the large airy houses of Miraflores. A servant in a gray uniform showed him into Tiburcio's study at the back of the house, then left him alone for a few minutes. He went to the large window behind Tiburcio's carved desk. Directly below him was the patio of the Jesuit school.

Tiburcio's oldest daughter came in with coffee on a tray. He had not seen this girl since Lilia's funeral. She must be twenty, he thought. She had not turned out as pretty as everyone had expected. She was healthy, however. All Tiburcio's children had a look of health and fertility. The girl left, and Tiburcio came in wearing riding boots. He sat behind the broad desk, tapping a quartz paperweight while Ordóñez drank his coffee. "So..." he said finally, "You see my daughter, Natalia. She has become a woman since Lilia died..."

"*Yes.*"

"She is a Peralta. She has Lilia's mother's eyes. So, my friend...so, my friend, you have conceived the idea of being a fiction writer..."

"That's not your affair."

"What is your business with me then?" Tiburcio went to window at the side of his desk, and drew back a curtain. A gardener was setting a border of coleus around the trunk of a silk cotton tree.

"It is," said Ordóñez, "that I wish to become a man of some small—some very small—means, in return for...ah... using, or not using, material that falls into my hands as a result of my...pursuits."

Tiburcio was silent. Then be said, "Yes, I see," and got up to open a file cabinet which stood behind his desk. Ordóñez looked out of the window at the gardener.

All I want to do at this moment, he thought, is to embrace Tiburcio. All I want to do is to take back my words so that I can embrace him...to clap him on the back and to talk of Lilia.

Tiburcio held out to him a sheaf of papers held together with a black string. "In the central mountain range, thirteen kilometers south of the town of Purificación. The ore tests at point six percent..."

Ordóñez could not speak. He took the papers without looking at them, and left.

THE *Americanita* had left coffee on the stove. He stuffed the papers into a desk drawer, still without looking at them, and sat on the bed to think.

Tiburcio had taken him seriously. Why? Why? Because of Lilia. Because of family. Not believed him, no! Simply made him a gift. Because of Lilia. He should have known this about Tiburcio. Tiburcio's message was that it was no good to love a whole land, a whole people. That had been his mistake. Loving a whole people undid your manhood. One must know how to cheat a farmer and love a cousin. Yes! Cheat a farmer and love a cousin. He rummaged for a notebook and wrote that down. Then he carried the meat pies and coffee into the bedroom, and wrote until past midnight.

In his mind was the constant thought that he would return the sheaf of papers. If it had not been for that thought, he could not have returned to his notebooks. As it was, the powers that moved the pencil were appeased. Ordóñez lives in a mud and bamboo hovel, his mind muttered. His oven is broken, and his bed slats fall on the floor during the night; his washing woman is an unbuttoned slattern, and his sister a pinch-mouthed shrew. His children sit behind the window grating, staring at the dusty street with empty eyes…

These were the terms. This was the pact with the power that moved the pencil. None if it could be changed. He looked up and saw that Dorie had set his books between two wine bottles she had filled with pebbles. He wiped it all to the floor.

On Thursday, he was absent from school. Dorie worried and left school on the early bus.

"Why can't you eat? She said when he turned away from the table without taking the soup she had made. You haven't you eaten all day."

"Of course I have. Stay out the kitchen and shut the door." He went and lay on the bed.

"What is it?" she asked.

"It is nothing."

"Then I'll leave."

But she did not leave. She sat weakly on the bed, fumbling in her pocketbook, intending to check to see if her visa was still valid, something she had been meaning to do for a month.

He was shivering and moaning. She laid her hand on his thigh. "Do you have a chill? I didn't feel well today either. There is another virus going around…"

He sat up in the bed and took her hands, cupping them over his face, and began to sob into them. "What is it?" she cried, "What is it?"

He spoke into her hands. "I have won that is what it is. I've won!"

"What have you won? I don't understand. What have you won? Why are you crying?"

He wiped his eyes on the sheet.

"Why do you shiver so? Are you sick? Felicia has had it too, and her head has ached for three days."

"Shut up," he said. "Stop talking and go to the desk…in middle drawer…take out the manila folder on the top."

"These papers with stamps on them?"

"Yes, yes, yes. Now don't speak. Hand them to me."

She brought them. "They are land titles of some sort…"

"Yes, yes, hush. I will look at them now."

"You have never looked at them before?"

"The deed…" he was speaking to himself, not listening to her. "The deed is drawn up correctly…yes…it is all in order…"

"What are you talking about, Paco?"

"…here is the lab report… copper, zinc, gold…"

"Paco!"

"Hush!" He did not look up from the papers. "The gold is high, high. It is good. It is excellent. If there is a road…I do not remember. Carambolos-Pura…I have never heard of a road. Give me the map! There! There, under those books."

"You have made such a mess of this room...oh, here it is. It's torn in half."

He spread the two pieces across the blanket, discarded the western half, and found what he sought in the eastern provinces. "There is a projected road! Carambolos-La Purificación. What is the date? What is the date on the map?"

She found it. 1961.

"Oh, but what is the use! A projected road is not a road you can travel on!"

"Surely in eighteen years..." began Done.

"There is no road! Shrewd! Oh, Tiburcio is shrewd!" He seized a notebook and began a furious calculation. Her head ached. "Could we have something to eat? I don't think the children have had their bread and coffee."

He held onto her hand so that she could not move away. After he had finished adding a row of figures, he said, "It is not such a problem as I thought. It is not such a problem as I thought, the business of the road. Even if I must take the ore out on mule back. I must still make five to six thousand a month, at the very least. Such a high concentration, with a riffle table, reducing it by half..." Then he was out of bed, bolting the door with the iron rod he used to protect against thieves and next he was kneeling on the floor with his head in her lap and his hands in her skirt. Dorie made one last effort.

"You couldn't possibly explain..."

"I have a chance...the last chance of my life, to become a man of some...small means, in short, a man!"

"Paco, explain!"

"I have a mine, in the central range, a gold mine. My wife's cousin gave me the titles."

"Is it far?"

"Far, yes. Carambolos, and then twenty kilometers on horseback. We will go. We will go, as soon as school is out!"

Ricaurte accompanied them as far as Charagua. "I wouldn't put principle into it," Ricaurte said, "but if this mine looks as good as you say, I'll put the interest on my Polar Beer stocks."

"We shall see, we shall see," said Ordóñez.

"In any case, I congratulate you," said Ricaurte.

"For what reason?" asked Ordóñez.

"For taking my advice on certain matters."

"Shut up, Ricaurte. As I have said before, you have no soul."

At the bus station, they parted. Ricaurte intended to take the mosquito plane in comfort. He would meet them in Fuencarral.

At Charagua a jitney was leaving immediately. They put off eating, and alighted in El Cambur at three. The ocean was visible from all the terminal windows. Ordóñez arranged for a room above a coconut vendor on the main street, facing the water. The room was whitewashed, and held a large bed with a straw mattress. The coconut vendor brought a metal table out to the sidewalk, then served them fried fish from his smoke-blackened kitchen behind the heaps of coconuts. They swam off a piling behind the police barracks, and lay on the black sand until it was dark.

"Tell me again. Say the words," she said.

"The mine is there, in the *cordillera*." He pointed toward the seaward slopes.

"Whatever is there, it is not good to talk. Bad luck "

"I'll say it then," she said. "Tomorrow we go to Fuencarral, and we stay overnight at the house of Francisco Trejos, who studied with you at the Christian Brothers and who has a *penca* plantation..."

"Ha ha ha! That was a joke!"

"What?"

"The *penca* plantation. *Penca* is simply a weed that grows on sterile land. A *penca* planter is a poor man, like Ordóñez. Poorer even."

"How does he live, then?"

"I don't know. I haven't seen him in sixteen years. Listen," he said, "No more telling ourselves stories. I do not know. I don't know where we are going, or what we will find. Only what is on the map. We go next to Fuencarral on the *Navales* tug, and to Carambolos, we go by bus. Francisco writes that there is a bus twice a day. I don't know any more than this." He lumbered over on to his back and closed his eyes. She sat up and put on her hat, afraid of too much sun. The Pacific was steely and sluggish under the diffuse sun. It was very hot, and they had to go into the water often to cool off.

"Fuencarral is in the mountains, you said?"

"The coastal plain. The mountains begin after Matamorros. Carambolos has an altitude of 2,000 meters."

"And Pura?"

"2,500 meters."

"And we must find a jeep..."

"Yes. The malaria unit is supposed to have jeeps, and the drivers will take a passenger, Francisco says."

"Otherwise, we will ride horses."

"Yes, or mules."

"Is there malaria?"

"Hardly any, in the mountains. There is simply a malaria control unit in every town. Almost two hundred thousand people are employed by the units. It's a good job. You get research grants to the University of Tulane, houses, jeeps, English lessons..."

"I see. I will finish," she said, and recited the thrilling words: "Carambolos has a population of fifty thousand. The area around Carambolos has rich deposits of silver, copper, tin, zinc...gold..." He was asleep, she noted

"You grow fat," he said that night, beside her on the straw mattress. "Almost like...

"Like what?"

"I should not say."

"I will say it then. Like *her*. You loved her..." The ocean, washing up almost under the wooden pilings, made her want to say these things right out.

"She was a...shape, beside me in the bed," he said. "I never asked myself: do I love her? After she was dead, I once saw a woman in a butcher shop. Her back was to me. I thought it was Lilia. She had Lilia's figure. I thought, if I could just take that woman who is buying an ox tail home to my bed—neither of us saying a word—perhaps then my pain could be eased."

"I like that," she said.

"What is that?"

"That you loved your wife."

He leaned over her. "The little weight is good," he said.

"I shall grow...monumental.

"You always have to talk," he said.

THE steel plate tug, named "*Si Diós Quiere*," carried the two of them and a choir of seminarians from Pastolagrande to Fuencarral. The boat was employed by the navy, but had time for one or two extra trips. Captain Trejos was careful. He'd once been scuttled by a party of drunken picnickers, he told them. "You, of course, are another matter," he told her several times. "I'm always glad to give a ride to your kind."

They docked late at Fuencarral. The sun was down. Trejos's woman had meat pies and beans for them. Ordóñez introduced her to them: "This is Dorie. She believed you were a *penca* planter."

Francisco Trejos served them small glasses of rum without speaking. After they had drunk, he said to Ordóñez.

"Are you married?"

"No."

"Don't tell them that in Carambolos."

"No?"

"You'll want credit. You'll want to hire workers. You know where my advice comes from, don't you?"

"Yes,"

"And all because I didn't want priests meddling. I've been faithful to her for twenty years."

"Doña Luz is a good woman.

Doña Luz didn't speak. She took away the plates, brought guava squares wrapped in plantain leaves, and coffee, then lamps which Francisco Trejos lighted with a candle on the table.

"Well, it's done with. It's done with my affair. Maybe you will profit," said Francisco Trejos. "Come, sit down in the other room. It was five, six years ago that Tiburcio was here. And it was sixteen years ago that I last saw you, my friend."

"It seems a year," said Ordóñez.

"Ha, man! That's a sign of age when the past comes back like the day before yesterday. But no, no, we are not yet old. Listen, I still have schemes. I will tell you about them."

"There is hope then. But first my scheme," Ordóñez said.

"Yes, yes, my friend."

"I am glad you remember when Tiburcio was here. It's important. I want you to tell me all Tiburcio did, what he found in Pura. I want to know why he gave up. You understand? I want to know why he gave up the mine."

"Why didn't you ask him?" said Francisco Trejos.

"Because I swindled him."

"I don't believe! *Ay hombre*, what pleasure you bring me! So, you are still a man of letters?" Trejos went on,

"Who is not a man of letters in this wretched country! It is a contagious disease."

"So, and Arturo Pino" asked Francisco Trejos. "Tell me, do you still meet?"

"Pino was in The Model Prison for a year. He is free now."

"And his newspapers?"

"He is forbidden to use the Postal Service but his paper is used to make up the weight on a private plane that distributes corn chips."

"Ah, magnificent!" exclaimed Francisco Trejos.

"Pino is known at this moment as Hippias Major."

"Hah!' laughed Trejos. "And you, my friend?"

"Ordóñez is no longer a political man."

"I don't believe…"

"This mine. What do you think this mine represents?"

"The redistribution of wealth? Ha, ha, ha!"

"No, no! None of our old phrases! It represents an act, an act! For a year, now, I have studied Tiburcio. I have four notebooks filled with Tiburcio's comings and goings…"

"And what have you learned?" asked Francisco Trejos.

"Simply, that it doesn't do to love an entire people."

"Ah…"

"Tiburcio cheats the farmers, gets the mineral rights under their lands but, to his own family, he is tender, benevolent, better than most men…"

"So you said you would publish your notebooks in Roberto Pino's publication unless Tiburcio…"

"Recompensed me with something of…substance, yes. That was essentially the deal."

"I see, you were prepared to…"

"To act. Tiburcio taught me how to act. I was dying, my dear friend, dying of discussions, of pamphlets and manifestos…but tell me now the year Tiburcio came…"

"Well, there isn't much to tell." said Francisco Trejos. "He came this time of year. A very dry year, like this. There were fires. In Carambolos the mountains burned down to the edge of town. Well, the Japanese, who had the mine before Tiburcio, had built two shacks, one for himself to live in, another where he kept the riffle table.

"Well, as I said, there was no controlling the fires. The shack with the riffle table caught fire one weekend while the Japanese was in Pura for the Day of the Dead. The stream nearby had dried up. There was nothing anyone could do."

"Was the riffle table destroyed?" asked Ordóñez.

"No, luckily. But the Japanese was at the end of his money. He couldn't even replace the shack. So he offered the mine to Tiburcio on the condition that the Japanese could stay on and run things and keep living in the other shack. It was agreeable to Tiburcio, and they spent the day with Judge Ramos drawing up papers. Tiburcio is a great one for papers."

"Was the mine working before the fire?"

"Yes, the Japanese had been putting one or two tons a day through the riffle table, and he had nine or ten mules that brought the ore into the railroad at Carambolos. So after the papers were done, Tiburcio got a roof over the table, and then he started working on the road. The old Doctor was helping him. You remember Doctor Restrepo, who worked for the government in Charagna?"

"Yes."

"Well," said Francisco Trejos, "he came to Carambolos to be part of the team that put in the hydroelectric plant and retired here. So he was glad to have little jobs like Tiburcio's road..."

"Yes."

"The road bed was halfway finished before he left. It will take a jeep or a unimuck. The Malaria Commission uses it. It's hard on jeeps, though." The lamplight faltered. Trejos turned up the wick. "And now you must tell me about the girl. Who is the girl?"

"She is a teacher, at the *Americanos'* school...I am a Spanish teacher there. All our children from wealthy families go to the *Americanos'* school now, so they can proceed to M. I. T. and desert their homeland...It offends but I work there. One could live well on the salary before the devaluation. It is a job...for years I could not get a job, because of a pamphlet..."

"And the girl has made you long for gold," said Trejos.

"No, no, she thinks nothing of the gold!"

"What, then, does she want?"

"Ah, man, adventure...romance. What can I say? Ordóñez has become a figure of romance. Ha, ha! I took her to my house. I was appalled! How had I lived so long in such filth and misery? I thought I was undone, you know, Franco. I could not even call forth my…manhood! But she was enchanted. She is one of those women who chooses to be engaged by…by a man's failings."

"Does she know how you…acquired the gold?" Trejos asked.

"No…no!"

"If it were not for her, would you be here?"

"Ah, perhaps not," he considered. "I…I was sunken in apathy, since El Cacique… We plotted…We plotted eight years to kill him, and he died, you know, in his bed…"

"Ah, yes. Of natural causes. I know, man. We, here, also had our cells and our meetings. El Cacique is our shame…"

Doña Luz brought in more rum, and a dish of limes.

"Drink up," said Francisco Trejos, passing the bottle. "How was your trip? Most people fly to the airport here. There's a mosquito plane from Charagua three times a week, now."

"Too expensive," said Ordóñez. "I am a poor schoolteacher. For three years I could not get work because of a pamphlet. Now I receive a salary one could live on, yes, when the *peso* was at ten to the dollar… Listen, did Tiburcio speak to you about the mercury separation?"

"Tiburcio, no. The old Doctor spoke about it. The gold content was high, he told me. High as he'd ever seen. But it's the devil to separate. "

"Yes!"

"The old Doctor said that if Tiburcio could bring in equipment to carry out a mercury separation and then ship the purified ore, he could increase his profits fifty percent."

"Yes."

"Trouble was the shacks."

"What shacks?"

"All up the mountainside above the mine. They've thrown up huts. Miserable peasants! *Penca* planters!"

"Ha, ha! *Penca* planters!"

"The officials wouldn't let the separation equipment go into the area. The fumes. They say Tiburcio would have to move all those people away."

"Ah…"

"Tiburcio did all the petitions. The papers, stamped and signed by the right people. You know that if it had been possible to do dirt to the *penca* planters, Tiburcio would have done it. There was a shooting one night. One of the *penca* planters killed his wife and another man. However, nothing was ever linked to Tiburcio."

Doña Luz carried a candle in from the kitchen, pumped up another kerosene lamp and lit it. "Come," she said to Dorie. "You are tired. I will show you your bed." Dorie followed her to the back of the farmhouse. There was no corridor and one bedroom led to another. In the first of these, a very young girl nursed a baby by candlelight. "My daughter," said Doña Luz. She showed Dorie to the room. "I will leave you a candle and some matches. Sleep now. They will talk until late."

RICAURTE came the next morning. They went by express bus from Fuencarral to Carambolos. Francisco Trejos recommended they stay in Carambolos, at the old doctor's place. They found the house just off the Plaza Central. Dr. Restrepo's wife, Consuelita, gave Ricaurte the study, and Dorie and Ordóñez got the room that belonged to her second son, who was away at the air force school in Malaganueva.

"I knew her at the Sacred Heart in Charagua," she told

Dorie as she unpacked their few things and stored them in a tall armoire, which occupied a third of the room. "Lilia was in first when I was in fifth. Tell me does he have children?"

"Yes, a boy and two girls."

"Three babies! Tell me, how old is the oldest? It is a boy? Ah, it is fine to have the boy first. And now he has a new wife. I am happy. And an *Americanita!* How do you like that, our Paco!"

He told her she must stay a day alone, while he went on to Pura to make arrangements.

"Why must I, Paco?"

"Consuelita expects you to."

"Oh, good Lord!"

"Trejos said we must be correct. He's right. There may be no place in Pura where a woman can stay. I'll have to look into it"

"One doesn't *count* discomforts, my dear," said Ricaurte that evening at dinner.

In the morning he walked with them to the Malaria Unit. It was early, not yet seven thirty but the market plaza was open. They went inside and ordered coffee. The woman behind a stand of dried beans served them the strong brew, sweetened in the pot, then occupied herself with stringing up market baskets. A child sorted lentils on the floor.

Ricaurte went to another stall and bought squares of white cheese, wrapped in a plantain leaf. "Fresh," he said, "Tastes of udder"

Ordóñez hurried them. "The Japanese, the hired hand, will be waiting."

"Is he going with you?"

"Yes."

She hated him. The terse takeover manner was not quite his style, and Ricaurte with his early morning gleeful face, making a fuss over some smoked cheese, was too much to bear.

They walked over to where the Japanese miner waited, seated on a soft drink case at the railroad station. He held a paper bag with ore samples which he silently handed to Ordóñez.

"It's high, high…," he said, spilling some of the contents into his palm…

"How many mules have you?" Ricaurte asked.

"Only five. Two old. Three die."

"How much is a mule?"

"A thousand *pesos*, a good one."

"How many workers have you?"

"Two, and the boy. The boy works for his food and bed."

The malaria jeep pulled up. "When will you be back?" Dorie asked.

"Late. About six."

"What will I do, all that time?"

"You will be with Consuelita. Her sons are gone. She will be glad to have you."

"Am I not imposing?"

"No. If you wish, go back to the market, buy her some fruit and a tin box of *petits buerres*," he said. Then he and the other two men got into the back of the jeep, which drove east into a deep gash in the red soil of the mountainside.

"**PETITS** *beurres*. How kind! You shouldn't have. Sit down, my dear, here in the patio with me. We shall have them right now." Consuelita pulled two wooden rockers into the shade of a row of rubber trees. "Betsabé, bring coffee," she called into the kitchen, which opened off the back of the patio. So your man has gone. He will be back. It is best you stay here. Pura is no place for a woman. Carambolos is a place where one can live. One lives in great contentment here. He tells me you are from New York. I have a cousin in New York."

"I am from New York State," Dorie said.

"Ah, my cousin lives on 8th Avenue. That is near?" asked Consuelita.

"No, far, very far."

"I see. She spoke to the servant. "Betsabé, put the *petites beurres* on a plate—one of the good ones from Doña Lucila's set. Lucila was the Old One's mother. She had fine things, from France. Everything from France. So kind, your little gift!" The servant wheeled in a brass cart with coffee and the cookies. The coffee was sweetened while in the pot and Dorie forced herself to drink it, as she gnawed at the grainy cookies.

"Your Mama, she is sad you are gone from her," Consuelita continued. "I know. I have three sons, all gone. The youngest has a scholarship in Charagua. The other two are in the military. I am alone with my Old One. But one lives very well in Carambolos. We have two cinemas and the *Club Social,* and the army barracks. Such a comfort, too, that the military is near… Bring us a bit more milk, Betsabé. You must have some more, my dear."

"No, no, I've had enough."

"You should try to eat more You are a thin little thing.

• 117 •

Lilia was always plump and strong, not a one to die...but then my son Sergio was not a one to die, either, so fat he was...

"You think of your man. You must be patient. He will he back. You are best here. In Pura a woman would be subject to indignities." Doña Consuelita patted her neck and shoulders with her napkin. "It is the hour of heat. We must go inside and rest. Perhaps you would like a book."

"Yes, please."

Consuelita led her into the darkened parlor where there was a glass-fronted bookcase. Among the engineering texts were a *Merck Veterinary Manual,* a copy of *Black Beauty,* in English, and a Spanish translation of *Eugenie Grandet.*

"Take anything you like," said Consuelita. "My son Roberto belonged to a book club. He used to read. We have a set of encyclopedias called *A Thousand and One Wonders of the World.* It has nice pictures. Maybe you would like to look at the pictures. It is so hot. One is too exhausted to read."

"No, no," Dorie said, "I will just take this" She took out copy of *Eugenie Grandet,* and, after going to the kitchen for a drink of water, she went to the room at the back of the house where Consuelita rested on a sheet spread across a day bed on the little balcony which overlooked the Carambolos movie theater. The Old Doctor slept on his rumpled bed, and Betsabé sat in the sun on the floor of the patio, setting her hair on cardboard rollers. Dorie lay down in her slip and, instead of beginning *Eugenie Grandet,* fell asleep.

When she woke, a clatter of bells from the church in the plaza was calling worshipers to six o'clock Mass.

Dr. Ruiz returned from a stroll to the post office and there was another sitting down to coffee. The old man consented to a boiled egg and Consuelita accepted an *arepa* with a bit of white cheese. They asked if she had slept.

"Oh, yes," she said, ashamed.

"Ah, but it is good fortune," Consuelita said. "One passes the bad time of day, and when one wakes the air has been exchanged."

The old Doctor explained. the noontime heat created a vacuum over the city, causing a rapid updraft later in the day and cool mountain air rushed down. E*l ventarón*. It seemed to be true. The leathery leaves in the patio stirred, and the tablecloth on the brass cart billowed.

By some miracle of the Postal Service, there had been a letter for her at the post office—forwarded by Trejos in Fuencarral—from Feli. Feli was coming to Carambolos on the eighteenth. She was touring the western part of the country with a North American, Tom Fleet. "A gringo who buys forests," Feli called him.

She found the letter difficult to believe in.

"How thrilling, we shall see your mine!" Feli wrote.

ORDÓÑEZ came at seven.

"Well, tell me"

"They've been robbing the Japanese," he said. "He had two men working the jackhammers, one to help with the riffle table, about sixteen carriers. There were several hold-ups coming down the mountain. The Japanese thought the workers planned them, or were working with the thieves. They may have been selling to the *Turkos*."

"So, what happened?"

"So he got rid of them. Does it all himself. He and the boy. Now he's selling to the *Turkos* himself."

"The black market?"

"Yes. They pay a thousand *pesos* more per ton than the

Central Bank but his. volume is down. He's only making enough to send a couple hundred to Tiburcio each month. Have you had dinner?"

"No. We waited for you. We'll sit down in a minute."

"Good," he said. "I must speak to the old Doctor."

"So, what will you do'?" she asked.

"Find workers. You can't run a mine the way he's doing it. The Japanese are like that, trust only themselves, eat and sleep on top of their business. He brings the mules in on Friday and sleeps under their bellies."

"But if the workers steal?"

"Even if they steal you have to have workers. They can't steal it all"

"So who will you sell to?"

"The *Turkos* for now," he said. "So, how have you spent the day?"

"I've read five pages of *Eugenie Grandet* and slept. Consuelita believes in the afternoon nap. Will I see the mine?"

"We'll hire horses tomorrow and go up. There's a place we can stay. A woman named Jesusa Solano. It won't be comfortable," he said. "Not like here."

"I hope not!" she cried passionately.

"ANOTHER mountain is burning," said Consuelita at dinner. "Above the military stables."

"No, it's not behind the stables but it's over toward the road to Pura, above where Betsabé says she sees the Virgin Mary," said the old Doctor.

"Ah, but it is a Virgin," said Consuelita. "We saw it today through Doña Lucila's opera glasses. She had a blue gown. She genuflected, and then turned to walk up the mountain, and then started to disappear..."

"By God!" said the old Doctor. "It's no Virgin. It's the shreds of a blue *Pisanista* flag left from the elections in 1951."

"There was no *Pisanista* flag up there in 1951, my love," said Consuelita firmly. "It is a Virgin. Isn't it so? Betsa?" she said to the girl, who had come in to remove the fruit plates.

"*Sí Señora,* it is a Virgin. Clarita sees it too, and Olga from downstairs."

"My God! It's a hysteria," said the old Doctor. "In any case, that's where the fire is."

"Run and see if that's so, Betsa. I'll finish serving the soup," said Consuelita, getting up. "We have bread soup tonight, my dear Paco. I hope you like it."

"Anything, anything, *Señora,*" said Ordóñez, who never noticed what he ate. "I'm certain it will be divine," said Ricaurte.

"So, my friend, did you have a successful look?" said the old Doctor.

Ordóñez nodded.

"I don't want to offend, but I have been wondering whatever put it into Don Tiburcio's head to give you the mine...," said the old man.

"I've been wondering myself, too...The mine is worth a half million a year. The Japanese has four lodes exposed, and no end in sight"

"God!" said the old man. "But the Japanese only sends a couple hundred a month to Tiburcio. I don't think he's crooked..."

"No, no! he's just foolish. Listen, to prevent an ambush losing him five or six hundred *pesos* worth of ore, he works the mine with one or two workers, or usually just the boy and himself. With twenty workers he could make ten thousand a month. With forty he could make twenty thousand. It's simple multiplication"

"Jesus!"

"A holdup is never more than five men," Ordóñez said. "They're outlaws living in the hills. They never put together anything on a large scale. Even if they steal the mules and all, and three or four tons of ore, it's a loss he can afford with forty workers or more."

"Perhaps you are right…"

"Are you going to tell me Tiburcio never thought of this?" asked Ordóñez.

"Tiburcio was worried about the mercury separation," said the old man.

"The devil with the mercury separation! A high grade ore with enough volume doesn't need to be concentrated in Pura!" said Ordóñez.

"Tiburcio has other investments. He didn't want to bother with it if he couldn't get the maximum return, that is the idea I have," said the old Doctor. "Besides it's dangerous selling to the *Turkos*"

"With more volume you could sell to the Central Bank."

"True…"

"Damn!" said Ordóñez, "You could sell to the Central Bank, take out an insurance policy for fifty million, station a guard…"

"You couldn't get guns."

"Tiburcio would have gotten them. It's what I say. Tiburcio must have realized

"Maybe so."

"Well then?" said Ordóñez.

"Man, Tiburcio has his ways. He is one for legal papers. Maybe the papers aren't straight," said the old Doctor.

"The papers are straight."

"You'll need money?"

"Yes. What do you think about it?"

"Well," said the old man, "I've forty-thousand in stocks of Polar Beer. I figure the government will go under before Polar Beer…"

"True."

"And another thirty thousand in Rosa Gonzalez's chickens."

"You won't see that again," said Consuelita. "Rosa's lost more than a hundred chickens. It's sunstroke"

"Sunstroke, no!" said the old Doctor. "Rosa didn't vaccinate. Imagine. Five hundred chickens and not vaccinating! Man, we'll see Arturo Pacheco who owns the laundry, maybe. What do you need?"

"I want about three hundred thousand."

"That's a lot!"

"Pacheco and who else?"

"I could talk to Enrique Lazo at the bank. And there's Consuelita's brother-in-law who had an investment in the mine at the time of the German before Tiburcio. I'll talk to them. We'll hire horses and have a little look. *Una miradita.*"

"*Una miradita que me hace temblar.* That was Carlos Gardel," said Consuelita. "Who was it that had that song on a record?"

"My brother," said the old Doctor. "He used to say our chief glory was that Carlos Gardel's plane crashed here, in the *Cordillera Central*. I was talking to him the other day, he said his son was going to study law because it was a career that could lead to many things. It was a 'good taking-off place,' he said. Alberto told him the best taking-off place was aboard an international flight at Las Charaguas airport."

"Oh yes, man!" Ricaurte laughed, pleased with the old man.

Betsabé came back into the room. "The fire...?" said Consuelita anxiously.

"The fire is on the trail to Silvia. The Virgin is safe."

"Ah, that is good, I couldn't think that God would allow a fire to take the Virgin."

"Ha! Or the *Pisanista* flag," said the old Doctor.

THE old Doctor hired three hacks and a steady mule for Dorie. Arturo Pacheco and Enrique Lazo came mounted on their own fine horses, which danced, impatient, on the pavement in front of the church. It was shortly after five-thirty. Bells clattered for six o'clock Mass. Ordóñez helped Dorie up and mounted one of the brown mares.

"Wait there a minute, Betsa's bringing meat pies," called Consuelita from the balcony above. She had a scarf on her head, preparatory to going to church. The girl came downstairs with a paper parcel of meat pies. Ordóñez put them into his saddle bag with the thermos.

Houses on Siete de Mayo Street were still shuttered and a few women were in the street carrying missals in string bags. Past another small plaza, the street narrowed, then became a country lane, which turned sharply left into the red cleft in the hillside.

They rode together until the guard post at the town limit, but Pacheco's horse was impatient. The old Doctor circled back to Dorie and Ordóñez. "There's a Polar agent just before you come to the plaza in Pura. We'll meet you there."

During the first half hour, the raw-red gash in the hillside continued on their left, with a crest of ragged grass about ten feet above their heads. There was an occasional shack with footholes leading up to it. To the right the terrain opened up. On an opposite slope was a *Polar* sign, lettered in white stones against the short russet grass. On a higher slope behind, *Llantas Goodyear*. The sun, settled and firm, now above the grassy crest of the cleft burned Dorie's left cheek and forearm. The mule's ears formed a V at the point where the road curved out of sight.

Nearing noon, they crossed a small valley and a river.

"The Pance River," said Ordóñez. "We will stop." They circled under a wooden bridge and stood in its shade while the horse and mule drank. A few yards from them, a muscular boy in a ragged bathing suit washed himself and his bicycle with a bar of green soap. *"Hola,"* he said. "Not much water." He indicated the slender stream in the wide pebbly bed. He accepted a meat pie from them and told them he was training for the Pura-La Floresta race.

"If I win that, I'll buy a new bicycle and enter *El Nacional*," he said.

They remounted. The road crossed a second, diminished river, then climbed again. The gash was on their right now.

She saw a small metal cross with a hub cap hanging on it beside the road.

"What is that?"

"A car went over," he said. She looked into the ravine below.

"Do they get the bodies up?"

"Not always."

"How terrible!"

There were a few mud houses, sun baked and crazed like

• 125 •

old china, with two irregular shuttered windows and a door. The thatch roofs were caught up on sapling racks and trimmed at the bottom like thick bangs. The windowless sides served as billboards. *"Hexamine:* PURGE LIVER AND GUT OF ASCARIS AND OTHER PARASITES."

The red cliffs crowded. The mule fell behind the mare. Another metal cross had a bicycle wheel draped over it. She noted the change in the vegetation. Here there were pines and blue-green eucalyptus growing out of the gorges, their tops at eye level. Rocks and tree trunks were charted with pale lichens. They stopped to put on wool ponchos. He pointed down.

"There's San Antonio below."

It was a village of white-washed houses, black thatch, a town square and a church. Walls, corrals, wandering borders of piled rock were bleached colorless as the grass. "Lovely," said Dorie, thinking how her nature went out to this austere landscape, while thinking she could never accept the sprawl and riot of tropical Conahotu.

Se Ven.

¿De Que?

So Café.

She read the sign in front of a shack. There, a woman in a black fedora refilled their thermos with coffee. "Is there cheese?" asked Ordóñez.

"*Sí.*" She took a large golden cake of cheese down from the nearly bare shelf. They stood outside in the sun to eat the pie-shaped slices. The storekeeper's child, also wearing a black fedora, touched the thermos.

"Will you give it to me?" he asked, and smiled at Ordóñez's refusal. "The knife, then..." He gave it to him.

"It is a poor knife," he said to her.

"And since we are to be so rich!" she laughed.

The road wound down to San Antonio, El Retiro, Pura. Tall eucalyptus crowded the valley below. Above, on the sterile slopes, were sparse rows of a spiky plant with wooly blue-white leaves and a russet bloom.

"Frailejones," said Ordóñez. "Little friars. They wear little sweaters to keep warm, the people say." The air was cooler, but the sun, directly overhead, heated their ponchos. "Are you tired?" he asked.

"No, I'm strong. In Warsaw I walked miles"

"Warsaw, *Varsovia*," he said. "Why is it called that?"

"I don't know. There used to be Poles, they say"

"We have, in Estado Cuayas, a town called Hollywood," he said. "The cities, they name in a fit of distraction but the small villages…it is like a father fastening his dreams on a child. 'Piety,' they are called, or 'Purity'…Purificación is a name given to little girls who grow up to be kitchen maids."

In the settlement of Las Cruces, storekeepers threw pails water on the streets to keep down the dust. The stalls in the market plaza were closing. Mangos and papayas rotted in the sun. From the billiard hall came the voice of Luis Barrios. *"Cuando tu te hayas ido."* The road dipped into a dry stream bed, then rose again. A wooden truck loaded with bundles of sour-smelling firewood was off the road with a blowout, and the driver was unloading the wood to lighten the weight on the truck. A woman with a chicken on a leash waited beside the truck.

The road rose, narrowing to just the two ruts worn down by the malaria jeeps. Then it doubled back on itself so that Dorie looked down and saw the disabled truck just below them. There were a number of abandoned shacks flush with the road, LIBERTAD PARA LOS PRISIONEROS DEL

CACIQUE was splashed up on them in fading blue paint.

"He died in his bed," Ordóñez said, "For twelve years we met and plotted, and he died in his bed." He said it mechanically, no longer in anger, but because it always stirred her toward him. Aware of this, he suffered a moment of self-hate. Aware, it is Ordóñez's curse to be aware...

The mountainside was burned off and sterile dusty *penca* weed grew, a paddle-shaped cactus, a few eucalyptus. Dry lizards twitched, dislodged pebbles, and stood immobile, staring. In the saucer-shaped hollows, where soil and sometimes water collected, there were always a few humped Zebu cattle. The shaggy wild burros stood nearly invisible against the bleached soil.

"There it is," he said.

Purificación lay below, a collection of thatched houses, four or five larger buildings roofed in corrugated gray asbestos. The road descended in two swings. At the elbow, the old Doctor and his companions sat at a metal table in front of the Polar agent's establishment. The tabletop was covered with empty bottles. Arturo Pacheco crossed the swept earth yard, which held the few tables set out for customers and a *bolas* court. He held horse and mule while they dismounted. "*Hola*. Misia Albertina has fried meat and soup. Shall we eat here first?"

"All right," said Ordóñez. "How long have you waited?"

"About an hour. Is the lady all right?"

"I am fine," she said.

"That is splendid. This soup has a nice face. You'll feel stronger." Arturo Pacheco slid two of the metal tables together, and brought chairs from inside. The drink seller's woman brought out the soup, thick and gray with plantain starch, fragrant with coriander. She had to push the plates in among the bottles crowding the table.

"Well, Ordóñez, they are talking about you," said Enrique Lazo. 'So the mine is going to run full again,' says that devil of a son of Artemo Upegui. He's wearing a soldier suit now and stands in the guard box at the entrance to La Floresta. The last time I saw him he was sitting in a wooden box in his mother's kitchen playing with a chocolate beater. I had to correct him, the fine young soldier; he thought it was Don Tiburcio who was back. Tiburcio hired his father as bookkeeper when he was here in 1947."

On the opposite side of Pura, the road was a single rut—the malaria jeeps did not go any farther. It bore left, past the mine to the village of Recife. Dorie rode slightly behind Ordóñez. The others quickly disappeared around a bend.

"Paco," she called.

He turned around toward her.

"We won't be afraid."

"No."

"Listen, could we have some motion? I want this mule to run, even if I fall off."

"Motion, yes. Hup! Ha! *mula!*"

THE old Doctor had brought pans to try their luck in the Culebra River. They crossed it at a shallow ford, followed it upstream around two bends, and dismounted under a large silk cotton tree. The old Doctor pulled the two steel dishes out of the saddlebags, wiped them out with the newspapers in which they were wrapped, and then sanded off some bits of rust with jeweler's cloth. Finally, he lit a stub of candle and ran the flame around the inverted pans until they turned blue.

"You ought to use the new plastic ones," said Arturo

Pacheco. "They're lighter to carry around, and you don't have to go to all that trouble"

"Been doing this since I was fourteen years old," grunted the old Doctor, handing Ordóñez one of the pans.

Arturo stayed with the horses while the rest of them walked down the steep slope to the stream bed. Ordóñez stopped her on a wide ledge above the water and showed her a bowl-shaped hollow filled with some rounded stones. "Look here."

"What is it?"

"The river rises in May and June and leaves these deposits. Sometimes they're rich in gold." He scooped up some of the gravel into a paper sack, taking his penknife and scraping out the crevices. "We'll look at it in the water."

He helped her down the step like ledges, until they reached the bank then they followed the river downstream until they reached a little pebbly beach. It was hot. She rolled up her pants and walked into the water up to her thighs. It was clear and rushed over the stones. Opposite her a Zebu cow stood in water to its knees, staring at her.

Ordóñez dumped the sample he had collected above into the pan and, wading into the water, submerged it. He bent over and mixed up its contents with the water. Bringing it up on the little beach, he washed off and threw away the largest stones. "I should have brought a sifter," he said. "It's been years since I've done this."

"How did you learn?" she asked.

"My grandfather was an old prospector. And I had an uncle who studied mines. He used to have a farm near here. We spent vacations there when I was at the Christian Brothers."

He went down to the river to submerge the pan in the shallow water again and began moving it back and forth just under the surface, allowing the current to carry off some of the muddy suspension. "Gold is nineteen times heavier than water," he told her, "so it will sink to the bottom. Most of this gravel and sand is only two or three times the weight of the water, so it stays nearer the top."

He lifted the pan out of the water now and began spilling the mixture off the top, shaking it from side to side, then spilling again. After he had done this four or five times, the pan was nearly empty, and he tilted it to show her the thin stratum of black sand at the bottom. "If there's gold, it's there," he told her. She felt an odd thrill. Gold, riches! It was an emotion she'd never felt before.

He added a little more water, swirled and spilled, until only the black sand was left. "There's color," he said, showing her the faint glitter. "Those crevices usually catch something when the stream recedes." He took a wax paper envelope from his pocket and scraped the sample into it, marking it "bank" with a felt pen.

They waded back into the water and walked upstream. He carried the pan balanced on his head. "Around this bend," he said. "You collect on the inner side of elbows. Behind boulders, too, or logs. They're all natural riffles and they trap the ore." Scooping up gravel near the back with his hands, he took another sample, then submerged the pan, agitating and spilling. She searched unsuccessfully for rocks.

There was no "color" in this sample. "What is that black stuff?" she asked.

"Mineral concentrate, chiefly magnetite. There could be some platinum. Heavy stuff: quartz, even gems." He scraped this sample into another envelope, and marked it "curve."

A few yards upstream, he dredged up some more sand and gravel and allowed her to try this time. "This uncle of mine," he told her as she swirled the mixture under water, "found a nugget the size of his thumb in the Chambur River. He never got over it, and spent the rest of his life in these hills. Whenever you saw him, he was carrying around a paper sack with ore samples. Wash off the larger stones now. And throw them out."

"Yes, that nugget left him touched in the head. He never found another. Took to drink, finally."

She lifted the pan and gingerly began pouring off.

"You don't need to be quite so careful. And keep the water moving," he told her. "He'd come around to our houses in the city, this uncle, and give us shares in his stake in exchange for a bottle of rum. Had them all stamped and ready, with a notary's seal and a red ribbon at the bottom. He must have given out hundreds of them. Keep it moving, now."

There was "color" in her sample. He showed her the minute flakes under a magnifying glass. "See the sharp angles, and the little bits of quartz still sticking to some of them? That means the lode is nearby. As you get farther downstream from the source, the particles get smoother. That's how the old men used to locate the lodes.

She found a boulder, and he carefully scraped the moss off it into the pan. "Best natural gold catcher, moss." They took turns panning this sample and it was backbreaking work.

Arturo called from the bank. "Did you get color?"

"Here and there," Ordóñez said, "We've got a good one here." He climbed out and showed Arturo the pan. The old Doctor came down the bank. He'd been collecting from an old stream bed, and held up a bottle for them to see. Dorie sat on the grassy bank and squeezed the water out of her pants. She watched Ordóñez show the old Doctor his wax paper envelopes. Oh my dearest, she thought, we won't be afraid. What was it he had said to her that time in her classroom? "My dear Miss West, we must be a little brave." Yes, we must be a little brave!

It was nearly three. They drank some of the cold mountain water out of a tin cup Arturo had brought and then they stowed pans and samples in the packs and remounted. They rode upstream along a narrow path that followed the river's course. Then the riders veered to the right, crossing a field of short grass crisscrossed by rivulets. Fat Zebu cows lay about like gray stones. Dorie twisted her fingers in the mule's mane and allowed him to bolt after the others. She was determined to keep up.

The trail returned to the stream and began to climb between buff-colored boulders. They followed an old stream bed to avoid the broken terrain, then scrambled out of it into a eucalyptus grove. Returning again to the river channel, they picked their way along its narrow bank, with its rushing water.

Once again, it widened to a broad stream with grassy banks. They crossed more treeless fields at a canter. "We're nearly there," he told her when they pulled up. Another field, more Zebu cattle, eucalyptus, *yarumo, a* few ragged palms. Most of the trees had been burned off by the yearly fires.

The path approaching the mine was nearly hidden by buff-colored grass. Ordóñez pointed to a deep hole from which a *yarumo* tree grew, with all but its russet crown below ground.

"*Guaca,* Indian grave," he told her. "It caved in twenty or thirty years ago, when Alfonso Barroso, a cousin of my wife's, kept a herd of cattle here. He dug it out, found a couple of nuggets. The lode runs this way." He angled hand and forearm diagonally across the buff hilltop toward a group of three mud huts, two roofed in thatch, one in zinc. A fourth building was roofless and abandoned. A red cur ran back and forth the length of his rope in the clearing in front of the largest shack.

The Japanese hired man was below, in a small ravine. They climbed down, using footholes dug into the clay. Halfway down was a scaffolding and the entrance of the mine, a ferrous red opening, seemingly propped open by bamboo poles. They stopped their descent, and the Japanese climbed up to meet them. Ordóñez shook his hand. "I brought the streptomycin for the mule," he said.

"The mule is recovered, *don* Paco," the Japanese miner told him. He was thin and rather tall. The creases in his face made him look like an Occidental.

"It's good to have it around in any case."

He crawled out on the shaky scaffolding and walked into the mine. The bamboo props marked off rough squares along a corridor which forced her to double over. No sign of gold. Of course she wasn't simple enough to expect that. The walls were red clay, like the outside. A network of split bamboo slats held back the earth. Her way was barred by a hopper which filled the entire corridor. She walked out again, and they descended the rest of the slope, alongside a wooden chute which carried ore to the riffle table below.

At the bottom of the ravine was a tributary of the same Culebra River they had been following most of the afternoon. It had been dammed up with cedar boards. Straddling the stream bed below the dam was the riffle table. On the bank beside it was a charred ruin of a hut. Next to it, a canvas roof had been rigged over the Jesperson ball mill. This was the only imported piece of equipment, Ordóñez told Arturo Pacheco. The riffle table had been made of cedar wood and zinc by a carpenter in Pura. The shack in which Tiburcio had carried out his experiments in mercury separation was now occupied by the Japanese miner, who had moved his domestic arrangements down the hill from one of the shacks above. It had a flat zinc roof with an *Eternit* cistern, and mesh screened vents all around the eaves. The disassembled tubing from the retort apparatus lay about behind it.

The Japanese wheeled one of the ore carts into the shack that housed the ball mill and shoveled its contents into the hopper. A greasy generator was out of its casing on the dirt floor. The Japanese miner knelt over it, while they crowded behind him, and guided a spark with his screwdriver. The ball mill rattled explosively for about ten minutes. When it stopped, the old Doctor picked up a handful of the milled ore that had filtered into the bin. Dorie looked in his hand, but could see nothing.

The Japanese, with Ordóñez's help, dumped the bin into a wheeled hopper and pushed it along a little boardwalk that bridged the dam above the riffle table. He positioned it so that he could dump it little by little onto a canvas apron at the upper end of the sluice. As he did this, he lifted one of the cedar boards which held back the water and allowed the stream to carry the material over the riffles at the bottom of the zinc sluice.

"He's learned to do it by himself," Ordóñez said. "But two men would be twice as efficient."

"My brother-in-law always swore by a rocker," said Arturo Pacheco, "You weren't always losing your ore downstream, and one man could handle the whole affair easily."

"Too slow," Ordóñez said. "You can't get any volume with a rocker. We aren't planning on a one-man operation, in any case."

The Japanese miner shut off the flow of water, then removed the canvas apron and washed it off in a trough. The riffle bars were removed in sections and carefully washed over the same trough. Finally, Ordóñez picked up the carpet that lay under the riffles and held it up while the Japanese washed it down with buckets full of water. The trough had drains which could be opened after the sediment had settled. The water which couldn't be drained off was left to evaporate.

In several other of these same troughs, which had already been drained, she could see the same black sand that had been left after the panning operation.

They walked toward the retort shack where the Japanese miner now lived. The slope on the opposite side of the ravine was not as steep as the one they had descended. At its foot was a stand of corn near harvest. Above it were orange and lime trees, which sheltered coffee bushes and even higher up were the shacks that had frustrated Tiburcio's plans. Why there? she wondered, thinking of all the uninhabited area they had traveled over. Then she recalled that wherever the soil was washed into these cuplike ravines, there were usually a few houses, cows, plantings...

Arturo Pacheco stood looking at the shacks. "I can't figure Tiburcio. *Penca* planters or no *penca* planters, there wasn't any need to process the ore here in the first place."

"That's exactly what I'm thinking," said Ordóñez. "He must have been imagining himself taking the Minister of the Interior through his establishment. 'Here, Don Roque, is the precipitator, and the sifter and the fucking condensation tower...The devil! Mules are what we need! Twenty-five mules and a large ball mill to replace that coffee grinder, and an imported sluice...or we can even do without that.

"The mules are the main thing. We'll take the ore out of

here in whatever state we must!"

Arturo Pacheco nodded. "You may be right

"I am right! If they rob us, they will have to carry off a lot of worthless soil as well as gold."

Enrique Lazo, who had been studying a handful of black sand, had not spoken. Now he said, "Do you think that is why Tiburcio gave it up…?" He gestured toward the shacks, "because he couldn't have his mercury separation?"

"Yes," said Ordóñez, "I am sure of it. Well, gentlemen, we will go in and have a drink. There is nothing more to see here. The story is in the samples…"

"How do the mules get in and out?" asked the old Doctor.

"There's a path over there." Ordóñez pointed to a worn furrow at the narrow eastern end of the hollow. "The Japanese thought of making an elevator. It could be done easily, just a platform and a pulley and the mules for power."

"Yes."

"We'll go back by the path. Wait," he said. He got a paper bag from under the riffle table, and held it open for Arturo Pacheco to sift his handful of ore into it. "Take it. It tests between 0. 4 and 0. 6 ounces to the ton at the laboratory in Gordas. See for yourself. The Japanese sent a sample to the United States, to Portland, Oregon. Same result. One ran 0. 8."

The eastern termination of the ravine was a sterile ditch, covered in the same bleached grass as above, its vertical gashes exposing layers of clay. They walked back toward the shack where the hired man lived. The sun was directly in their faces. The Japanese pulled a table out into the yard, and brought out a bottle of rum and some small glasses. Dorie asked him for coffee, and walked into the shack to watch the water he put to boil on a kerosene stove. She sat on a folding chair, noting that he lived amid a remarkable proliferation of objects: three cots were crowded into the corner opposite the kitchen, two of them made up with print bedspreads, the other covered with oriental dolls. The rest of the room was inexplicably, filled with electric appliances, all new, many still in boxes, but there was no electricity. A niche over one bed enshrined an Osterizer under the bed she could see three automatic fry pans. She wondered which cot he slept in. Or perhaps he slept in none—Ordóñez had said he slept under the mules' bellies—so as not to disturb the print spreads and the dolls.

A set of pink plastic dishes was drying in a vertical wooden drainer. The Japanese took out a cup and saucer, and set out the coffee on a Polar Beer tray with a dish of crackers. She wanted to sit outside, but he took a print cloth cover from a leatherette armchair and indicated she should sit in it.

"I will go outside with the others."

He shook his head. "No, sit here." He poured the boiling water through the cheesecloth bag into the cup. She sat down, thinking of the oddity of the Spanish language hanging there uneasily between them.

"You are very comfortable here," she said.

"Yes, quite. Many thanks to the *Misia*. The *Misia* takes sugar?"

"No, thank you. It is a pretty set of dishes," she said.

"I buy in Lagunas. *Contrabando*," he said. The word passed like a dirty penny between natives, was handed gingerly between them.

"All things..." he waved his hand around the room, "All things I buy in Lagunas. The *misia* does not use sugar?"

"No, never."

He frowned and went out to the men.

After they'd finished the coffee, Ordóñez took some of the sediment from one of the troughs from which the water had evaporated. Tying a bandanna over his face, he poured a few drops of mercury into it, swirling the little globules through the sand. "The mercury makes an amalgam with the gold," the old Doctor explained to her. Ordóñez kept shaking the pan, adding more mercury until he had a single puddle of amalgam. The Japanese miner then held a chamois cloth out to catch the ball of amalgam as Ordóñez tipped it out of the pan. Then he squeezed the free mercury out through the cloth into a bowl and returned it to the vial.

In the meantime, the old Doctor and Arturo Pacheco had set up a Bunsen burner fueled by propane, and a condenser, made out of an old bicycle pump, attached to a retort. This was to separate the gold from the mercury, a process Tiburcio had planned to carry out on a larger scale. Ordóñez sealed the ball of amalgam into the small steel pot clamped over the burner, and heated it while the Japanese poured water into the condenser. He waved them back as the mercury vaporized, for there would be fumes escaping from the makeshift seals.

The Japanese, wearing a pair of asbestos gloves, detached the retort from the burner stem, carried it to a water trough and plunged it in. When it was cool enough to handle, Ordóñez unscrewed the top and showed her gold, still molten. Again the novel emotion, like a tickle of gold. Will we be rich? He poured it into a vial and put it in his pocket.

They left the ravine by the opposite, more gradual, slope, and circled back to the animals.

𝕁𝔼𝕊𝕌𝕊𝔸 Solano was pouring Lux-Cola on a small blaze in her parlor when they arrived. A candle stuck in a saucer had fallen over and ignited a small pile of laundry. A servant with a sullen face hung back in the shadows.

"God! Augustina, the whole house would have burned if I hadn't come!" she exclaimed, then looked up and saw them at the door. "Come, come in! Look at this!" she waved the bottle of Lux Cola. "No water, no water in the house! If I hadn't happened to have had this...!"

She turned to the servant. "Go to the kitchen!"

Ordóñez finished stifling the smoldering clothes with one of the charred diapers. "A very dangerous thing..."

"Yes, yes, of course. My heart is pounding! She did not stick the candle in the saucer well and then she left the room. You must excuse me. Come in, *Señora,*" to Dorie, "I will attend to you immediately. First I must clean this and then you shall have a beef steak and some plantain. You must excuse me..."

"Don't upset yourself for us," Dorie said.

"Ah, but what a thing to happen! You are guests! Wait, wait there while the smoke clears. I will bring you a chair to sit in the entryway."

Ordóñez went to tether the mule and mare in the small plot behind the house. She sat on the rattan chair Jesusa brought out to the front garden that looked across the dusty street into a small plaza opposite, where four men played soccer in the last light. Jesusa brought her a dish of *badea* pulp. "I will have something hot for you soon," she said.

"There is no hurry. It is good..." The cottony *badea* was like a compress laid on her dusty throat.

"The cursed girl, she is packing her suitcases," said Jesusa.

"Will you make her go?"

"No, it is her idea to leave me, in the middle of supper. She has nearly burned my house down, so she must leave. It is very logical!"

They both laughed. "Ah, my dear!" gasped Jesusa, embracing Dorie. "What can be done...? What can be done?"

Ordóñez came back into the house. "The supper, I must get your supper," Jesusa cried and returned to the kitchen.

"The servant girl is leaving," Done explained to him.

"This minute?"

"Yes, she is packing. I'll go in and help. Paco, where shall we sleep?"

"The front bedroom. She will sleep at the back, with the infants. Her man is at the barracks at Guaduas." He began to cough from the smoke. "Let us walk outside a moment." They crossed to the plaza, and sat on a broken bench.

"You saw it, this afternoon?" he said.

"The gold, you mean? It doesn't exactly knock one's eye out. I didn't expect that, of course."

"You should not have looked at Ricaurte's hand. Rather in his eyes. His eyes said, 'Ordóñez has gold!' I saw it there. It is the highest emotion after all...this..."

"This what?"

"This possessing!"

The black-and-white soccer ball rolled toward them. He picked it up, and drop-kicked it back. "To see the others' envy," he continued. "Ha! I was calm, wasn't I?"

"Very calm. But I don't understand."

"The other is off his balance . Envy puts one off balance. To possess is to be calm."

Jesusa's older child stood before them. "The supper is served," he said in a grave voice. They walked back. Only the white cotton pants of the soccer players were still visible in the plaza. In a large silk cotton tree at the corner of the house, cicadas trilled and dropped their tiny excrement like rain.

Jesusa served them fried plantains and meat, along with rice warmed over with beans. The infant was slung across her shoulder in her wide blue shawl, leaving her hands free. When they were finished eating, Dorie went with her to the kitchen.

The concrete sink was filled with dirty dishes from several meals. On the kerosene stove, several sticky pots had been set to boil in order to loosen the deposits of food. "Damned Augustina! She has left me all the dirty pots hidden in the oven."

"I will help," said Dorie.

"No, no, you should not."

"But I want to. I have nothing to do."

"Ah, you are a good girl. How long have you been married?"

"Not long."

Jesusa's mind was still on faithless Augustina. "Tomorrow I must send to the seamstress to help me find another. The priest could get me a girl, but my man doesn't like me to go to the priest. There are some girls that pass in the street every week. They usually don't ask over fifty *pesos* a week, but they steal and they don't have health papers. Augustina had her health papers, at least, and bathed. She was not a bad girl. They get frightened. Once I said to her, 'Augustina, have you seen my stockings?' I had misplaced them and I meant nothing! She burst out in tears and began tearing the house all apart. God! All the drawers were on the floor. Then she brought out her cardboard trunks and unloaded them all on the patio for me to see: missals, underwear, magazines, all her accumulations for me to see. 'No stockings. Augustina does not steal stockings.' 'It is no matter,' I said. 'You will get the police!' she screamed.

She could go to the devil I told her and went to play canasta to calm myself. When I came home she was dropping tears into a mess of parsley on the cutting board. 'Even the soup will taste of your poison,' I said. 'You have poisoned the day with so much misery!' Ach! I will be alone. It is better." The infant in the arms of the oldest child began to sob and hiccup. Jesusa took it and wrapped it in her shawl, and slung it behind her shoulder.

"I could stay," said Dorie abruptly. "I could help you."

"Ah, my. little one…," Jesusa laid a hand on Dorie's cheek. "You are welcome to stay. I have no one but infants for company. Infants and the venomous Augustina. How happy I would be for some other. But you must not work. God! You embarrass me!"

"Is your husband in the camp?" Dorie asked.

"Is that what they told you?"

"Paco told me."

"Yes, he is in the camp."

"I must tell you, Jesusa, I am not married to Paco."

"No? Ah, well…my husband is not in the camp. Neither is he my husband. He is father of the children. My man. He left before this one was born, and went to the camp, it is true but three months ago the officer came here to look for him. God knows where he is…"

"Do your boys go to school?" Dorie asked.

"No, the government school won't take them until they know their letters. I have tried with the older one, but he is a vagabond. He will not learn. And, with the infant, I do not have much time."

"Listen, I am a teacher. I'll stay and teach him!"

Jesusa laughed. "Such a short time, such a short time and we are sisters. Will he let you stay?"

"He will let me. I will tell him he must."

Augustina came into the kitchen with a tin trunk and two cardboard boxes, which weren't yet tied up. "Here are my things. See that I have stolen nothing."

"To the devil with you and your boxes! Get out of my kitchen!" hollered Jesusa. The infant began to cry again.

The girl was pale and dignified. "Idelfonso is coming for me in his taxi."

"OK, ok." Jesusa turned away and began scraping loose the burnt food on the bottoms of the boiling pots. The brother, pale and slight like sister, came in and tied up the boxes. The two went out. "God go with you," Jesusa called after them. "I have no rancor. I am not that way," she said to Dorie.

DORIE lay on top of the spread on the big bed, too tired to undress. Ordóñez went into the bathroom to prepare the aspirin solution Amable Rosero advised as a contraceptive. My body gets heavier every day, more receptive, she thought. Soon all this *coitus interruptus* and aspirin water will fail...

He returned, and put the syringe on the night table. "I am thinking," he said, sitting on the edge of the bed, "I am thinking that the idea of a heaven and a hell is not very satisfactory. It does not please mind or spirit..."

"What a thing to say!"

"Pardon?"

"A strange topic," she said, "But tell me…"

"Transmigration simply seems a more advanced idea…"

"Transmigration?"

"Yes," he said. "At times one becomes quite happy, convinced one's wandering, body-free spirit goes on, comes back…at the level of one's highest…vision. It is a beautiful idea…"

"Yes."

"I sat talking once. It was in a bar in Charagua. To a journalist I had known. He had come from hearing Myra Hess play Mozart; she performed one concert in 1950, on her way from Buenos Aires to New York. He, my friend, was a lover of music. He said to me, 'This is as high as I can go. Let me start from here next time around.' His face was the center of a field. He might have been thinking of a Second Coming! Ha! I thought, this is the way I want to die…composed, sober…but not too sober! Ha, ha!" He took off his clothes and lay back on the bed. "Must I undress you?"

"I like it," she said. "I think of that first time, with my costume…"

"The costume of the many buttons."

"Yes."

"You cannot offend me." She got up and took off her clothes. Their candle was only a stub. They let it burn away and drown in the last wax. She shuddered after he had barely begun, having been waiting too long. "Forward female," he murmured. Her fatigue was gone when he had finished, but he lay sleeping. She lit another candle, used the aspirin solution, and then watched him sleep. His sleep was her reward, though sometimes, when he woke after about ten minutes, he touched her gently, and spoke of their intercourse. "It is a good thing we have. I become accustomed to your body."

More often he woke with his mind on something else.

"I cannot sleep in this bed," he said as the second candle was going out.

"You were just asleep."

"It is too wide, too soft."

"It is strange. You're so monkish."

"Yes, I am monkish. Yet just now, I dreamed of satrapies." He sat up and spoke into the darkness. "I am thinking now, suppose it is true, the opposite..."

"What opposite?"

"That instead of coming back at your highest...you, you are reincarnated at your lowest. The gold, it is the gold. I feel I will never sleep again."

"I'll stay awake with you." she said, lighting another candle.

But he immediately fell asleep again, and she watched another candle drown in the saucer.

Just before dawn they both woke.

"Did I call out?" he asked.

"I don't know," she said. "Perhaps you did. I woke."

He sat up. "A vision of hell! I feel the whole night I've been trying to call out and have had...no voice, no voice..."

"It was a nightmare," she said.

"No, not a nightmare. There were no monsters, nothing to frighten. Only ordinary things. I was having my hair cut, someone was selling me a mule. Yet it was Hell. Hell has visited me for my talk of reincarnation. I tried to call. I did call out at the beginning, for Lilia, for my dead mother. And she, one of them, came to me. I lay on a wide bed with my son Luis beside me. We were both wrapped in a sticky web. She, Lilia, told me the Devil had entered through a broken pane in the window. 'It will be all right,' she said. She hung bright-colored ornaments all over the room and dangled them from the web, the sticky web that bound me."

"A dream, just a bad dream," she said.

"No, no, it was then the horror began. I was in a cafe, with Tiburcio. He was selling me a mule and it was Tiburcio selling me a mule. How can that be so full of terror? Yet it was.

"Tiburcio was speaking English. He took the deed from his pocket, the *titulo,* to the mine. He handed it to me. 'Here is the deed. It is yours now,' he said, in English, in English it has two meanings...deed.

"Yet it was...such an...ordinary thing. Why did it frighten me so? Why did I seek to call out and have no voice? Then I saw. Lilia had been right. It had been the Devil who entered. I recited the Our Father like a child who does not know the meaning of the words. Again and again, thinking, let me wake, only let me wake out of this...then I woke. I was saved...

"I was saved. It was terrifying, terrifying. It still makes me tremble. I cannot believe this room is here, that I could come back."

"Please, please, try to forget it," she said.

"I used to detest waking at this hour. It meant insomnia. Now, now it is a salvation. This room, that window, whole and sound. The armoire...I want to embrace them."

The armoire with a mirror front, and a sink in the corner of the room were becoming visible in a gray light.

"Lilia could not save me. Lilia was a saint. She had nothing, yet she was happy. It made her happy to read in *Bohemia* that Lolita Alvarez had a fur-lined bath. She could not save me. She hung tinsel wreaths..."

"Forget it, Paco, please!"

"How can I forget it! One does not feel a presence so strongly more than once or twice in a lifetime...!"

"I'll go and make coffee. We will get up. It's the only way." She got up and dressed in yesterday's pants and shirt.

"You will see. It will pass."

Jesusa's infant began to cry.

She went out to wash in a basin in the corridor. At the back of the house, Jesusa stirred and cursed. It would be all right, she thought.

ORDÓÑEZ went for the mule and mare. She waited, shivering, in the yard. He came back wet from the dewy plantain leaves. The day, it seemed, would be sunny.

"Where did the others spend the night," she said.

"It depends how long they drank, I would say that they slept over at the mine." He threw burlap sacks over the backs of the animals, then the saddles.

They circled the little plaza, then took the trail to the mine. "Why are we going back?" she asked.

"There is a belt I need to replace on the mill. I must take it off to see if they have a similar one at the *Casa del Pueblo*. Yesterday I forgot..."

"And then?"

"Then, to Carambolos. Where else would we go?"

"Paco, I want to go for my clothes, and come back, to stay with Jesusa. I don't care what Consuelita thinks."

"With Jesusa Solano? You are not thinking straight."

Dorie kept up to his fast trot. "I want to and I shall do it!"

He slowed the mare. She saw she had won. "I have nothing to oppose you with," he said, "seeing that I wake in

• 148 •

this...condition. Do as you like."

"Paco, what condition...?"

"Can you not see?" he said. "I am not whole."

"Not whole...?"

"Be silent, please."

They climbed the left fork, the single trail, to the mine. White sunlight dazzled her eyes. She felt less fear of falling as they went uphill, so she kicked the mule to keep up. He momentum carried her downhill again to the shallow valley where a few shacks hung off the slopes. At the end of a bamboo aqueduct, a woman was filling a red plastic bucket. Several washes were already stretched out to dry over the bougainvillea vines. What difficulties men make, she thought.

She drew up beside him. "My dear..."

"A miserable, divided creature," he muttered. "That is Ordóñez."

And how relatively simple it can seem to a woman, she thought. "Listen," she said, "Let's not go now." At once she knew exactly, what they must do. "We will give it up. We will give up the gold. It has made you something different from the man I wanted." Her mind was cleared of all that had happened in the journey here. She saw him on his bench in the plaza with his notebooks, in his bed at home with students' papers spread across the Chibcha spread, at the ditto machine spinning out his seditious letter...The man she allowed to unbutton her many buttons.

"No, no!" he said, kicking the mare. Reckless, she allowed the mule to gather his legs under him and to canter to the next rise. She lost one rein and tangled her hands in his mane. God in heaven. What a performance! The path lost itself in sparse grasses of the barren tableland. A few shacks were there, too poor to have a morning wash, or a bicycle leaning against the porch, *penca* planters. A man, sitting on a bench in front of a sun-crazed mud facade, called.

"Hola, Don Tiburcio!"

"Buen día," Ordóñez said, not noticing the mistake. They passed on. A few seconds later the tableland shook with a small explosion. Dorie looked around quickly, "What? Where?"

She noted the man was gone from the bench into the dark doorway of the shack with neither bicycle nor morning wash. Then she saw Ordóñez's mare fall to its knees and saw him tumble over the neck of the mare onto the pale earth.

Her speed carried her past him. She turned back as rapidly as she could and dismounted.

"My dear, my dearest…!" He was on his side, knee drawn up. The mare seemed to be dead. "What can I do! What can I do!"

"Come closer," he whispered, "Closer!"

She bent over him.

"Examine me, now, as if I were dead."

"Dead!" she cried.

"You must! Cover me now. Cover my head with the blanket…"

"No! No!"

"Otherwise, there may be more to come…"

"Oh, my God, oh my God!"

"Do it now!"

"Yes, yes…I understand." She straightened his legs, and placed her poncho over him.

"Then ride on. Don't go back, just go on. Get the others. They will be at the mine…"

She went. There was no one in front of the shack any longer, only the blackened doorway. As she rounded the last curve, where he had pointed out the *guaca* the day before, she met the others. Ricaurte was trotting at the head with an eager morning face.

T**HEY** loaded him on Arturo Pacheco's horse as if he were a corpse and brought him back to Jesusa Solano's house, where they laid him on her bed. Then they continued down to Carambolos for the doctor. Meanwhile the pharmacist from Pura brought gauze, penicillin, and morphine.

The wound was in his thigh. The leg lay at a terrible angle, but Jesusa said they must not touch it. The fever began at midnight, and Don Emilo came again with more penicillin, and *Conmel* for the fever.

Late in the afternoon, the doctor from Carambolos came with Ricaurte in the malaria jeep. Dr. Ramos. He took care of medical emergencies in Pura and Recife, hitching rides with the malaria people.

It was a difficult wound. The bullet had entered at the top of the thigh and passed out near the knee. Tendons and muscles were torn, and the bone splintered. Ramos bound it to a board with gauze, and told Jesusa to raise the leg on pillows. It could not be put in plaster, he told Ricaurte, until the inflammation subsided. *Ambramicina* every four hours, anti-tetanus, morphine. "Does he have money?" the doctor asked Dorie.

"I do." She took a five hundred *peso* bill from her bag.

"It will do for now. I will tell you when you owe me more," he said. He would come back on Tuesday. "There will be swelling and odor. It is to be expected."

On Tuesday, the fever was high. Ordóñez passed the night restlessly, fell asleep at six in the morning. Dorie sat most of the day in the kitchen with Jesusa, drinking cups of the brown sugar water which bubbled all day on the kerosene stove, ready to add to the milk formula which the infant drank. It was a cold misty day. Dampness permeated the kitchen, which was open on one side to the back patio where Jesusa kept hens. Jesusa stood at the stove tending the pots of boiled beef, beans, rice, which served for both lunch and supper. The infant was kept lulled, slung across Jesusa's hip in her large blue wool shawl. At intervals it was fed broth from the cooking beans and meat, or rice water with the sugar water and milk. Dorie twice took broth into Ordóñez, but he would not eat.

"The penicillin doesn't seem to do any good," she said.

"Let the fever work. The fever has to work," said Jesusa.

"It is hard for you, with the girl gone. And now this," said Ordóñez.

"I have been without a girl before. They know when trouble is coming, Luisa Restrepo, my friend, says. They get out before," said Jesusa.

Dorie was wearing one of Jesusa's cotton dresses. She had washed her underwear, slacks and shirt, but there was no sun to dry them. "Can I take the child so you can rest, or go out?"

"I suppose I must go to Mass. I will go at quarter after four, in time for the elevation. That will satisfy them, and the boys will not trouble you for being just ten minutes late. Then I must pass by Magdalena Street to turn in my lottery card. I will be back at five."

"Yes, yes, I will watch everything."

"Okay. When the rice is done, put the meat back on the flame, and if the beans run dry add the beef water, yes? You must not worry." Jesusa inclined her head toward the room where Ordóñez slept. "The fever must work. I will light a candle." She handed over the infant who, it seemed, was never put down. The child cried. "Give her rice water. She is a little off today. The bowels are loose. Give her only the rice water, no milk. Good! I go now. Joselito, Federico, have you combed your hair and tied your shoelaces? If you have not, I will leave you here. Ach, Joselito, you are filthy! You shall not go and you shall not have an ice at the *Turcos*. Come, Federiquito." Joselito lay on his back in the patio, howled, kicked over a rubber plant in a ceramic vase.

"Ah! Come then and let Father Ricardo see what a beast you are. It is four-twenty. We will not even reach the Elevation. Give me your shoe." The child continued to lie on the floor, he held up his feet to his mother, who broke a lace in fury.

"That is the end! Heavenly Father!" She left with Federico. The boy continued to lie on the patio floor. "It is not my fault. Stupid mother!"

Jesusa put her head back in the doorway. "Little heathen! Stay there and howl!"

The weather had cleared, and there was a square of sunlight on the patio floor. Dorie went to the bedroom for her wool poncho, then lay it on the floor and set the baby down in the sun.

"She will get a cold," said Joselito.

"No, it is warm. Come see," said Dorie.

"I like it here."

"Okay."

The infant did not cry, so she went to the laundry room at the back and brought out her shirt and the underwear she had washed the night before, along with the sodden diapers Jesusa had taken in during the noon showers. She stretched as many as she could fit on the floor, and hung the rest over the low wall. Joselito moved closer. "Son of a whore mother.

I would rather go to Mass with Augustina."

"Your mother has many worries."

"Is the *Señor* in there dying?"

"No, but he is very sick."

"Could I look at him?"

"If you do not speak."

Joselito went through the kitchen to the front room, then came back quickly.

"He is awake. He made a face."

"Will you watch the baby if I go?"

"Okay."

"What can I do, Paco?" asked Dorie.

"It pains me."

"There will be the drug at six. Can you wait? Will you have some broth?"

"No broth."

"You must keep up your strength."

"No broth."

"Don Emilio will be back tonight with the doctor. It's a matter of waiting for the inflammation to subside. There is nothing to worry about..."

"Don Emilio, yes...I...begin a thought on this plane, this plane of pain...finish it elsewhere. I saw Lilia in a star...beautiful, young..."

"Your fever is high."

"...and Ricaurte leading a parade in a drum major's hat. Ha! With a baton! And a man on a bench. '*Hola, don Tiburcio*,' he said."

"He mistook you."

"Mistook me? No, there was no mistake."

"Paco..."

He was asleep.

In the kitchen, the rice was cooked. She moved it off the flame, and put the meat back to boil. The infant cried. Joselito had taken away the aluminum pans she had given her to play with. "Why do you do that?"

"My mother will not like it."

Dorie picked up the child who smelled very bad. She changed the diaper, then carried the soiled one to the laundry tub. While the infant screamed, she went to the kitchen for rice water. The square of sunlight had climbed the whitewashed wall. She hung the half-dry diapers over the low wall. The child took half the bottle, and fell asleep. Dorie lay beside her on the bed, and also slept.

She woke to the sound of rain on the patio floor, a gurgle of drains. Talking in the kitchen were Jesusa and the pharmacist, Don Emilio.

"Poor child," said Jesusa when Dorie came into the kitchen.

"Has he had the sedative?" she asked.

"Yes, the doctor was here and he changed the bandage."

"I wanted to see, to offer help."

"You need to sleep," said Jesusa.

Don Emilio was seated at the kitchen table having broth with shreds of the boiled beef in it. Jesusa served Dorie a bowl of the same, and set a bowl of rice and fried plantains between them. Federico and Joselito sat on the floor in a corner, scraping their metal bowls. Since Augustina's departure, they all inhabited the kitchen like servants. The infant was back in Jesusa's shawl.

"Is the fever still high?" Dorie asked.

"Yes, it is working. The fever must work."

"He is sleeping," said Don Emilio. "Sit down, *nena*. Eat."

He piled rice in the center of the thick broth. 'It's good, Jesusa," Dorie said.

"Yes, good. I am a better cook than Augustina. Damn! She was poisoning us."

"Augustina Peralta? She is from a good family," said Don Emilio.

"Yes, they are the worst. The mother worked for me after the father was killed. The child was called Luz Estela then. The mother kept changing her name. The child was being taught to play the guitar by Oscar Lugo, the famous composer of *boleros*. She was going to enter the Miss Estado Arango contest at fifteen and save them all with the prize money.

"When she was twelve, the mother brought her here. She had finger nails three centimeters long and had painted her face. And the mother, with her cheeks rouged with saffron powder like a savage! Estela, the girl was called then. She used creams. God! There was a portrait of her in the window of Fotos Diana in Carambolos."

"It's true, there was," said Don Emilio.

Jesusa shifted the child to her other hip. "She went about like a ghost, 'a spook,' my man called her. She didn't want to break her finger nails and went about the house dusting like a fairy and she would never touch meat, Miss Estado Arango."

"Too pale for a beauty queen," said Emilio.

"Yes, the mother would have done better to make her eat. 'Thin Soup', Luisa calls her. My Federico is pale from her cooking. I will cure him," Jesusa said.

"Still, they are good people," she went on. "The brother works hard, owns his own taxi. He keeps the mother now that she's old. Yes, if Augustina wants a reference, I will give it to her with pleasure. She might work for gentility. We are not gentile here!"

"You are a good woman, Jesusa. Nothing is ever said against you," said Emilio.

Jesusa barked a laugh. "Don Emilio, you sit in too many kitchens to tell me that big lie! You have your little coffee at Luisa's, and your little chocolate at the priest's…your little injections here and there…"

Don Emilio shook his head. "At Luisa's there's nothing ever said against you, Jesusa."

"Yes, Luisa's loyal. It's true."

"And the priest is a sick man."

"That is so?"

"A liver tumor. How the man deceives himself! He said to me when he had to go to bed last week with the pain. 'Don Emilio, isn't it just my bad luck to be down again with this little intestinal influenza?' Didn't I think the doctor should try some little vitamins to build up his resistance, he said. I felt his abdomen. There are three great tumors. It is a miracle there has been no obstruction."

"Ah, that is so? God forgive him. He is still getting about. He was at Luisa's yesterday. He and Luisa and Marta Aparicio have five-eighths of a ticket in the Christmas lottery. It will fall in Estado Arango this year. It was Guayas last year and Ensenado the year before. Marta says if they win on three numbers, they will go to Miami and bring back dresses for our little business. As you know, we already have the six Parisian dresses Luisa and I bought from Uriel Cruz in Manzanares. I had no money to put on the ticket but they cannot leave me out, as the Paris dresses are half mine."

"The priest will be dead by Christmas."

"And he doesn't know? He will have made no arrangements to avoid the death tax?"

"A man can deceive himself to the very end. Pepe Vegas was in Carambolos Clinic with tubes, tubes in, tubes out, strung up all over the room, and a priest outside the door. He was asking me if I thought it was a good idea to buy sheep to put on Leoncio Restrepo, his brother-in-law's, farm in Recife."

"But Pepe Vegas was not a man to see his money go to the state."

"No, that is so." Don Emiho stood up, closed the black leather valise, which held his syringes and needles. "It has stopped raining. I will go now. Many thanks."

"Thanks to you, Don Emilio," said Jesusa.

"One moment," said Dorie. She went to get fifty *pesos* from her bag. Don Emilio took it without looking at it. "Don't worry. Your man is strong. The more fever the better. It's the little fevers that are cause for worry. I will be back at ten tomorrow. Take care."

"Yes, Don Emilio. Good evening now," said Jesusa.

Joselito was asleep against a potato sack. Jesusa carried him to bed, then came back to feed the infant. The room was full of her odor. "Ah, I forgot to tell Don Emilio to bring some binding powder. No matter. The rice water will do. Don Emilo is a good man: a respecter of women. He is around with Luisa and me and the priest. It is his life but he has no family. The priest tells him to marry me, but I wouldn't have him. I am too young for that sort. Don't you agree?"

Dorie laughed. "I don't always understand you, Jesusa."

"Yes, yes you are not, not where you belong."

"I feel very happy here, however."

"Yes? That is marvelous! Such a life."

"Tomorrow I will teach Joselito his letters. I must have something to decrease the fever to…"

"Yes, my darling, you must not think of it. And Joselito will mind you or I will beat his head."

The rain began again. There were no more candles. They went to bed.

At midnight, Dorie woke from a weak dream. "Water," Ordóñez repeated, this time to her conscious mind. The moon lit the patio. She went to the kitchen without a candle, found a tin mug and filled it from the jug under the drip stone.

"I will not be able to sleep more tonight," he said.

"Why not? Are you in pain?"

"No. Only thirsty, I had a dream…"

'Is that why you can't sleep? I don't understand."

"An urgent dream…the man with the gun…"

"He mistook you. Tiburcio had injured him, not you."

"I must think. It was important!"

"But one doesn't give such thought to dreams. It was a business with your wife's cousin, anyway. Nothing to do with you."

"With me, yes, with me!"

"But a dream," she said, "how can a dream…?"

"Listen, listen! Tiburcio was in his study, with the glass-fronted bookcase carved in Manzanares for his marriage. He handed me a deed, the deed to the mine. 'Here, take it,' he said. 'It is a valid deed, made out in the notary's office, with five fifty *pesos* stamps affixed.' There was another paper on the desk. He handed me another…another deed…"

"Paco, please…"

"Another deed, also notarized. With three stamps of ten

pesos each. 'Here,' he said, 'This also, you must take over from me...You must assume it,' were his words. 'It is my debt. Yours now.' His deed, what he did to those poor *penca* planters is what he meant. Yours now...mine now."

"Paco, can't it he forgotten...?"

"My *deed!* In your language it is expressed by the same word. Ah, the symbols, the symbols lie deep. You wish to share in my property, he was telling me, you must also share my guilt..." He was becoming hoarse. "Give me water please."

She went to the kitchen again. 'The sky was full of fast-moving clouds. The wind had dried the patio.

"'It cannot be forgotten," he said. "It is full of meaning."

"Not now, then, let it go. Rest."

"Now. I must make sense of it now."

"What sense can be made of such a thing? A man sits in front of his house with a loaded rifle beside him, waiting for your wife's cousin to ride by so that he can shoot him in the back. A fine thing! How long did he wait?"

"Tiburcio was here three years ago..."

"What could he have done...have done to that man?"

"Tiburcio took what he wanted. It was his nature."

"Beautiful nature!"

"Beautiful, yes! Symmetry...Grecian...a fine plot plucked out of chaos. There are few enough...few enough such fine plots. We must attend to them. Apply our intelligence. My notebooks. I do not have my notebooks here..."

"Paco." She felt a stir of resistance. "There is no justice in it."

"No, no justice only symmetry is necessary," he said.

Then laughter rose. This absurd man, she was choosing

him again. But could she endure it?

"It's nearly four," she said. "I must sleep, Jesusa will need me."

AFTER breakfast, Dorie washed her hair in the shower stall made of cement blocks behind the chicken coop. The patio was full of mid-morning sunlight so she pulled a kitchen chair out into the middle and loosened her hair from the towel. Going through her shoulder bag, intending to count her money, she found a felt pen and an old, half-used exam book. With these she decided to write a story for Joselito the blasphemer.

He hung over her watching her draw large letters.

"Whose name is this, here?" she asked.

"Mine, Joselito."

"Which part is *Jo?*"

"*Here, Jo, Jo, Jo. And se, and lito, and se again and here. Sienta...Joselito se sienta en un asiento!*"

"You have read it all. You told your mother you couldn't read."

"I write too." He grabbed the pen: *Joselito malo*, he wrote.

"Why? Why did you tell her you couldn't?"

"*Puta Mama, puta Mama!* Here I will write it and a picture too!" He wrote the words, drew an evil Joselito.

"A devil!" said Jesusa from the kitchen, where she was giving Don Emilio coffee.

"A son should respect a mother," said Don Emilio.

"Thank God he doesn't know what he's saying yet," said Jesusa.

"I know what I say," said the boy. "Ha! I know what I say!"

• 161 •

The doctor came at eleven. The wound was fetid and draining but the swelling and fever were down.

"You owe me a thousand pesos now," he said to Dorie.

"Yes," she said. "What I have in the bank will cover only half. I can give you an IOU and try to pay the rest in September."

"An IOU from an unknown person, I cannot take."

"But don't be like that!" cried Jesusa. "She came here on a pleasure trip. How was she to know this misfortune would happen!"

"I could get a statement from my employer," Dorie said.

"Has he no money?" the doctor asked.

"No, no, not that much. He has a family. I don't wish to trouble him."

"I cannot accept an IOU. I, too, have a family. The *Rurales* pays me a laughable salary…"

"What can I do?" said Dorie.

"Put him in the charity hospital then."

"No, no, he would die there," Jesusa said. "My cousin and my uncle died there. I would lend it. Oh, I would lend it if I had it!" she cried. "There must be someone, the priest, Luisa…"

"The men who were here with us, the old Doctor in Carambolos, Mr. Pacheco, were going to lend Paco money for the mine but I don't like to ask them. It was a delicate matter. Paco would not like…

"Wait!" She suddenly thought of Feli. "What is the date?"

"The sixteenth," said Don Emilio. "I, too, would…if all my money were not all tied up in some calves…"

"On the eighteenth or so they were to be in Carambolos, my friend…my friend and someone she's met…"

• 162 •

"Who, who is this?"

"My friend, Feli, and some man she's met…someone who buys forests…"

"North Americans?"

"Well, yes, that is he…"

"*Norteamericanos!* Of course they will be *Norteamericanos!*" cried Jesusa. "She is herself! Who would not take a check from her? Blue eyes! She has blue eyes! It is scandalous!"

"No, no," said Dorie, mortified. "It is all right. This friend will have cash. He travels and he buys forests."

"Of course he does." Jesusa affirmed complacently.

"Ah," said the doctor. "That is quite satisfactory."

"I knew there must be a solution," said Don Emilio. "Impossible that there not be a way, some way. Now we are all happy!"

"He buys forests, you said?" asked the doctor.

She nodded.

"He would have business with Maderas Prensadas, then. There is an agent in Carambolos. Maderas Prensadas is connected in Charagua with Maderas-Clapperton."

"Excellent," said Don Emilio. "An excellent connection."

"It will be satisfactory," said the doctor.

"She has blue eyes!" continued Jesusa, berating the doctor. "The Devil himself would take a check from her!" She juggled the infant. "I am ashamed!'"

The doctor grunted and asked, "How does he seem, in there?"

"The fever has been down for a day," Dorie said.

"Ah, ha!"

"But he feels that pain more now."

"It is natural."

"And he dreams," she added.

"What is that?"

"He dreams, day and night, and wakes in fright and cannot forget…"

"I know nothing of that," said the doctor. "Listen, I must tell you, it is very likely he will be a cripple."

Dorie nodded. She had feared this.

"Does that concern him? Has he spoken of it?"

"No, he talks only of the dreams."

"I know nothing of that," the doctor repeated. "But such a wound, such a wound as his would have had surgery…repair in Charagua. There are tendons and muscles destroyed. I am not a surgeon. There is no one in Carambolos who could have repaired such a leg. Perhaps something can be done later, perhaps not…"

"I see."

"Will you tell him?" the doctor asked.

"I don't know. I doubt it will interest him."

"How can that be!"

"As I said, his dreams are all he cares about."

But after he had left, Jesusa said, "That doctor is a shit."

Dorie laughed. "We won't worry about it. Joselito and I read a whole book today," she added.

"Ha, ha," said Jesusa. "I was the same way. I just looked at the words in a book one day, and I could read them. I was four years old. No one had ever taught me anything, except that I was a girl and had to keep my thing covered…"

"It is a rare thing. I'm a teacher and I have some knowledge."

"Of what use is a woman's brain? Tell me that!"

"Jesusa, I love you."

"Yes, my darling. You are upset. It is the business about

the check. I told you, he is a shit."

"No, no. I was upset only about what you said, actually."

"What did I say? If I should ever offend you…if I should ever offend you, I would beat myself…!"

"No, no! It was only what you said about the blue eyes…"

"But it was not meant to…"

"No, no, you meant nothing bad and it is only that it is such…cheap praise, Jesusa. I am not responsible for my countrymen being able to pay their bills. Maybe most of them pay their bills, but I may not always. I love you, Jesusa, and you look on me as some kind of marble bank."

"It is a terrible weight, the weight of one's country, yes," Jesusa said.

"No, no. Listen! I do not make airplanes, or computers, or Fab soap. I cannot understand the simplest of these matters. I do not wish to claim them. How can you lay them on me?"

"You will claim them. Anyone would," Jesusa said.

"No! No!"

THAT night Ordóñez got up. Leaving his leg on the bed, he swung himself into a chair at the side. From the chair he managed to pull toward him the exam book and felt pen that Dorie had left on the table. When she woke, he was writing rapidly in the book by the light of a candle he had melted to the arm of the chair.

"Paco, you mustn't! What is it?"

"I'm writing a letter"

"No, no! You must lie still."

"I am writing to Tiburcio. I must tell him. I am breaking

the pact"

"What? "What pact? I don't understand."

"The gold"

"You know, you never told me. You never told me anything. How did this gold become yours? Why are we here? You have never told me."

"The gold is not mine. I have given it back. In exchange for my notebooks. Now I must have an envelope." He folded up the piece of paper on which he had been writing.

"In the morning," she said. "You must get back in bed"

"I cannot. I must sleep here. I have found a bearable posture."

"Well I suppose I couldn't help you by myself anyhow. We must have Jesusa or one of the others to help." She couldn't understand how he could have moved himself, how he had borne the pain.

"The pact is broken." he murmured. "I return the deed. That is what I have told Tiburcio. We shall be as we were before."

"How were you before?"

"He, Tiburcio, the whole man, ha! In love with himself, capable of acts cruel and necessary and I..." He grimaced and moaned.

"What are you?" she asked.

He could not answer for a time, groaning and writhing. Then he muttered, "I am the antagonist, the necessary antagonist. I must have my notebooks back."

She was silent, trying to understand. "You are...necessary to each other...?"

"'Yes, yes. I am writing to tell him I am writing to tell him that I must return to the self that I was...in order to fight him, you see... But I don't regret, I don't regret what has happened. A bond, this leg, a bond between us. But now...I must give back the deed...give back the deed in exchange for the notebooks..."

"I don't understand."

"In exchange for giving me the mine, I told Tiburcio I would never expose him in the press..."

"Ah..."

"Do you see now?" he asked. "I blackmailed him."

She frowned. "Why did you want the gold, Paco? Why?"

"To feel myself...a man. I might have done it," he added.

"Yes, yes, you were fine," she said. "You were grand...but I was frightened, remember? I didn't want to go..."

"I had to go."

"Yes, I understand," she said. "Yet it's wise, I think, to know when you don't want to die."

He looked at her as if just becoming aware of her presence. "You should not be here. It's no place for a woman."

"But I am here. I had to know, to see...as much as you."

"I don't know, I don't know..." He was tiring. "Tomorrow you will mail the letter. Yes, that's good and now help me back."

His arms were weak. Even with her straining to lift him he could not move. "I cannot. I will stay here until Don Emilio...I am exhausted. I will sleep here."

But he slept just a few minutes, then woke again. It was nearly four.

"Are you in pain?"

"No, no pain, just weakness, yet I cannot sleep."

"I see you have filled my notebook. You're welcome to it," she said.

He laughed. "It's quite a satisfactory notebook."

"I was using it to teach Joselito to read. But he knew. He knew already. There was nothing to teach."

"It sometimes happens, though it's rare. You tell a child the letters once and he remembers them, he has such a desire to figure out this reading. Perhaps he'll be a great scholar."

"No, he is too disobedient. But he'll be something special."

"Perhaps el Presidente de la Republica! Hah, ha!"

"It's a long while since we've laughed," she said.

"It's true. Gold makes one solemn."

"Are you comfortable?"

"Yes, I am happy. I am thinking, if I have my notebooks back, the things I can accomplish…"

"That's good. You feel happy in reality, not in dreams."

"But it's the same thing. That is what I have discovered."

"I don't know…" she said doubtfully.

"You would not know, of course. I didn't know either, before. A dream is a preparation."

"I don't understand"

"For what one must do next. Like giving something up."

"The gold?"

"Yes, I have given it up. Truly. It will go to a greater scoundrel than Tiburcio and they will say of me as they said of Cervantes. 'He died in want.' Ha, ha, ha! The schoolteacher, Ordóñez, he died in want."

"I loved a man who sat on a bench in the Plaza Central between two stacks of notebooks…"

"Ah, Warsaw, you are my good girl. But now I must sleep. I must sleep. My dreams wait." He sank back into the chair.

"I'm a bit jealous of your dreams," she said.

"Ah, Warsaw…"

"Of your dreams…of all of it!" She was crying. "I am jealous, yes, I am jealous."

"Ah, Warsaw, Warsaw, you must not be. You must not be."

ON Thursday at five-thirty, she rode back to Carambolos in the malaria jeep. She sat in back on one of the wooden benches, facing a sullen young man injured in the arm by a machete. In the front of the jeep, Dr. Ramos discussed with the malaria worker a herd of *Zebu* cattle crossed with Herefords, which he had recently put to pasture.

"They are four months old. Beautiful! They are resistant to everything: heat, drought, and flies. Not one has died. It is the *Zebu* strain. They could live on a snow cap. And they are fat, almost as fat as pure Herefords. Cross breeding is an excellent thing. If only one could do it with people and introduce here the North European strain. You would produce a people with craft and resistance on one hand, and enterprise on the other. Beautiful."

The malaria driver took the rutted road at great speed, blowing his horn at each curve. The boy with the wounded arm groaned several times. Ramos passed him a canteen of water and two Colmel tablets. He continued whimpering in a lower tone, his head bouncing cruelly against the metal crossbars.

It was dark when they reached Carambolos. "Check at the Hotel Lindbergh tomorrow," Ramos instructed Dorie. "Your friend will be staying there, I imagine. If he took the mosquito plane from Tres Reyes, he will be in Fuencarral by ten o'clock. He will probably hire a car from there and be here about noon."

They left her off at the old Doctor's. Doña Consuelita, Ricaurte, and the old man were at dinner. "Sit down! Have a bit of this nice rice," said Consuelita. "I will have Alicia make another chop, or will you have an egg? Ricaurte has just ordered a little omelet."

"No, no," said Dorie. "I will just have dessert with you, and some coffee."

"Doña Consuelita treats one like visiting royalty," said Ricaurte. "One has a continual dyspepsia…"

"My dear man…"

"Ah, but a dyspepsia one would not forego for any reasons of temperance!"

"Poor child, tell us how you are," Consuelita said to Dorie.

"I am fine."

"And he, how is he, our poor friend?"

"He is making progress."

"But, my child, you should have come back here. Pura is no place for a young woman like you. See how thin you are!"

"I am well. I had to stay. It was not bad there."

'But one worries. A woman in Pura. Here we are so well off, so comfortable. We have everything: two movie theaters, a town club and a country club, and the *Junta Social* that brings in entertainment from Charagua and even from Buenos Aires. And we have doctors and two clinics, besides the state hospital, and the military. One feels so much more at ease. Yes, but you will stay here now. We will fatten you up again. Lilia was always plump. It was the way he liked her."

"No, no!"

"But he is recovering. He is being seen by the doctor. What more can you do for him? Here we shall take care of you."

"I will see. First I must see my friend's friend. They are coming. He buys lumber, trees. I must see him about borrowing some money. He will be here tomorrow maybe."

"Yes, *nena,* yes. Now you rest. Go to your room. I will have something sent in." Consuelo rang for the servant. "There is a disagreeable breeze this evening. I shall go to my room, too. Make us a little lemon tea, Alicia, won't you? I feel I may have an indisposition coming on. Bring a little cup to my room and to the *Señora.* Go now," she said to Dorie. "You will feel better with a little tea."

Dorie slept in her clothes, on top of the spread, the way she had become accustomed to in Pura during the many nights of little sleep. In time the tea grew cold beside her. In the morning she avoided Consuelita and washed out some clothes at the back of the kitchen. At ten, she went for a walk in the park and checked for Feli at the Hotel Lindbergh. There was a reservation for them, but no time given for arrival.

It was an old hotel, built largely of wood. The lobby was filled with cloudy mirrors, reflecting each other. Spindly wooden columns held up a high wooden roof with a skylight.

She went into the dark dining room and ordered soup. Only one other table was occupied, by a group of domino players. The waiter disappeared into the gloom of the corridor and returned with a cup of pureed vegetables.

"Can I have bread?" she asked. She was struggling with a sense of disappearing into cloudy mirrors.

"Certainly, *Señora.*" He took it off another table. She couldn't eat the soup, but munched bread and drank water, then coffee. She was ordering a second coffee when Feli materialized at the table.

"Dorie? Yes! Goddamn, you can hardly see in here. Yes, it's you! My God!"

"The man at the desk told you I was here?"

"He said someone, some woman...but, my God! Tell me, tell me! What goes on?"

"A great deal goes on, but sit down."

"What are you doing? Eating lunch? Here's Tom..."

Dorie stood up. "I wasn't really eating..."

"Here's Tom," Feli repeated. "Tom Fleet."

She shook his hand. He was large and fair.

"This place is awful," he said. "Let's go across to the *Turkos*. We haven't had lunch."

They sat at a table on the sidewalk in front of the Syrian restaurant. Tom Fleet had a beefsteak. Dorie dipped bread into a bowl of pureed chickpeas. Feli didn't eat. She stared at Dorie.

"I must look terrible," Dorie said. Feli looked sleek beside this large man. She was wearing yellow slacks and a black and white polka dotted blouse, with her hair in a yellow chiffon scarf. "I just couldn't believe in your letter you know," Dorie said. I didn't believe till just now I saw you come in."

"You've lost weight," Feli said.

"Maybe I have, yes. But I'm well, I've been well..."

"But where is Paco? What about the mine?"

"Yes, yes, I'm going to tell you the whole thing,"

And so she told, starting with the money for the doctor, working backward to the shooting.

"Oh, God!"

"A bit of excitement, yes..." She was skirting tears.

"But will he be all right?"

"Yes, though probably lame. He doesn't seem to mind about that however."

"Doesn't mind?"

"It's difficult to explain. I don't think I can get you to understand," Dorie said.

Tom Fleet spoke for the first time. "He'll have to give up the mine, of course. There's no law enforcement up there, and once one of these things get started…"

"Yes," Dorie said, "But that isn't what troubles him either." She recognized Tom as something Feli had promised herself, like the nose bob in Switzerland.

"What then?" Feli demanded.

"I can't explain…"

"Good Lord, Dorie!" Feli stared at her, gaining substance from the large man beside her. While she, feeling herself becoming more insubstantial by the minute, decided to get her business over with while she could still carry it off.

"Listen," she said. "I need the money for the doctor."

"How much?" Tom asked.

She had to keep herself from looking away from his face and recalling afternoons she prepared hot milk and coffee for Lily and Rita, pulling off the skin from the milk in the brown, chipped pitcher. They are mine now, she thought, and I must fight for them.

"Fifty thousand *pesos* would take care of what we owe now and probably will be owing. Would you have that?"

"Over at the agent's I would," he said. "I could get it by tomorrow."

"I can start paying you back in September." She closed her eyes on tears.

"Ah, ah, you poor thing," Feli said.

She began speaking again, without looking at either of them. "I had to come with him, you know. I had to see it all. And I did, I did see it all…the town, the mine, some kind of…giant device they had there, that rattled. Maybe a little glitter of gold even and then, that shack—the poorest shack you ever saw—with a man sitting in front on a bench, at seven-thirty in the morning, with a rifle in his lap…"

"Oh, God, Dorie!"

"And the terrible thing was, I had to leave him lying there, and ride that wretched mule to get help."

"Did you go back to Pura?"

"No, I went on ahead to the mine. I met the three men who had gone up with us coming back."

"And they took him to Pura?"

"Yes, to the house where we had spent the night, to Jesusa's. Ricaurte came here to get the doctor. He had fever, terrible fever, and dreams…"

"You look awful," Feli said, "Just awful."

"And then the dreams, Feli. He had all these dreams, day and night, and they took him away from me. I couldn't follow. He left me all alone…"

"Look, Dorie, suppose you come back with us."

"No! no!" Feli had taken off her sunglasses and Dorie looked at her powdered face, the dark skin under her eyes, like a bruise which she always carefully made up, searching for her vulnerable friend who came late for the school bus every morning. This man couldn't have entirely changed her, could he? No, she was Feli. This was Feli, not *doña* Consuelita trying to take her away…

"Oh, I don't know, I don't know," she wailed, forgetting the presence of Tom Fleet. "If he would just say, 'Stay, stay, I need you…'"

She got up. "I'll go now. I have to get some sleep. I'll let you know. I'll let you know…"

SHE slept poorly, woke to a clang, clang…tintintintin, the second call for Mass, mimicked by the caged bird in the kitchen. She went out on the balcony and the servant was on her way to Mass, a lacy wing on her head.

She couldn't think of the name of Feli's young man. Two syllables…Tom Fox, Jack Box, Bob Flat, Jack Sheet… The molar, which had not troubled her in a month or so, was beginning to throb. Of course, she thought, a bad tooth does not cure itself.

Coffee was on in the kitchen, and the breakfast things laid out on the tea wagon, awaiting the girl's return. She heated the milk, tinted it with the black elixir and stood in the patio drinking it. The old Doctor rumbled in his sleep. Of course, a bad tooth does not cure itself. She felt with a finger, and found a swelling on the gum.

Tin…the last call. She had no idea which Mass it was. Her watch had stopped at 4:30. I am letting everything go. She rinsed out her cup and went up to dress.

The Maderas Prensadas agency was closed. She saw the Hotel Lindbergh casting long shadows, and thought it must only be seven or so. Eleven o'clock, said the clock in the hotel. Seven-thirty, said a boy delivering bread.

Should she call Feli? She would be asleep. Should she go back to the house? Stay and wait? She sat in great agitation on a bench in front of the hotel. I must stop this, stop this… she thought. Tooth thumping, heart thumping. She felt she could not live another hour. How could this be? In the space of a day for everything to fall to pieces…?

She walked slowly back to the agency. Still closed, she continued walking along the broken sidewalk leading to the market plaza, skirting a row of Syrian merchants who were setting racks of dresses, belts, enameled bowls out on the street.

Above their shops was a dentist: Raul Medina Zacour.

She had climbed the stairs before she realized she had no money, only the useless checkbook...

"*Señora?*"

She collected herself. "Perhaps you can give me an appointment..."

The woman looked in her book. "Four o'clock tomorrow. All right."

Dorie took the card, ran down the stairs quickly and out into the street flanking the market, waving off dark arms offering oranges, green mangos.

What shall I do...? What shall I...

Then she saw the Japanese miner, sitting on a burlap bag, sorting lentils. "Ah, Missus Dorie," he said. "You are waiting for jeep?"

"Yes, yes," she said. "When does it leave?"

"Hour," He held up a bunch of the stubby purple bananas that tasted like apples. "You like...?"

"Yes, thank you." She took one. "Listen," she said. "How much does it cost to have a tooth pulled?"

"Ten *pesos* at the *Rurales* but you wait long. Seventy-five *pesos* regular."

"Could you lend me...?" she asked. "I will pay you in Pura."

"Okay," he said, and handed her a bill for one hundred.

She shook his hand. "You are so kind. I will be back, okay, in less than an hour..."

"Okay," he said.

She returned to the street of the Syrian merchants and again climbed the dark stairs.

"I have only an hour before I must leave. Could he pull my tooth now instead of tomorrow?"

"I will see," said the woman in the corridor. She went inside, closing the door behind her. As before, there was no one sitting on the benches lining the walls.

The woman returned. "Yes, he will do it. You pay now."

Dorie handed her the bill. "That is seventy-five, isn't it?"

"And twenty-five for the pills," said the woman, putting the money in a drawer. "You can go in now."

There was no one inside the office, either. The appointment for the next day had been a formality. She sat in the chair with her eyes closed, not wishing to see if the dentist was dirty or criminal, but he spoke softly, kindly. "Do you want gas or Novocain?"

"Novocain," she said. "I have to travel in an hour." She endured the needle, then sat alone again in the room, feeling sleepy and a bit restored. It amused her to think that no one knew where she was— not Paco, not her mother and father, nor Mr. Hillyer, nor Tom Fleet, nor Feli. Only the Japanese miner and this Syrian dentist.

"You have a fistula beginning. I will give you some capsules."

"Yes."

He went to work—a powerful man, his abuse of her jaw perceptible only in the hardness of his fist against her cheekbone.

Then it was done. He handed her an envelope of pills. She shook his hand. "Thank you, thank you," feeling an overwrought gratitude.

ORDÓÑEZ was sitting up in bed, bathed and combed when she entered the little back room. The priest and Don Emilio were playing *lulo* with him at a card table drawn up by his side. "You look fit," she said, noticing his pallor,

• 177 •

the sag of his jowls, the reduced bulk of his body for the first time.

Jesusa brought in a tray of coffee. "It's fresh," she said. "And I brought meat pies on my way from church. I try to tempt his appetite."

"Yes," said Dorie. "He must eat."

"They come every day to play with him. It cheers him up. Yesterday he won seventy *pesos,*" Jesusa said.

"That's good," Dorie said. She remained in the doorway while Jesusa poured the coffee for the men. The priest could scarcely contain his glee over the pile of red beans he had won. "He's theirs," she said to herself. "A man in a setting."

"A man in a setting." Her own words to Feli back in those days after the Carnival. I was forgetting what I always knew, she thought.

"Come," Jesusa said to her. "We will sit in the parlor, like ladies." She carried the tray with what was left of the meat pies into the little room they hadn't used since Augustina's departure. "Tell me, how is the old Doctor, and Doña Consuelita? Do they drink their little coffee, and take their little naps, and go to see their little movies, as always?"

"Yes, as always."

"How many years has it been now, since they came to Carambolos? It must be twenty-five years at least, and nothing has changed for them. 'You can live well in Carambolos,' Consuelita always says…"

"Yes."

"I have a girl to help in the house. The priest sent her over. A mere baby. Thirteen years old, at the most. She is smaller than Joselito, and she can't cook anything but rice. But it's something. She slops the floors after a fashion, and carries the baby when I go to the market."

"So you don't need me anymore," Dorie said.

"You ought to stay in Carambolos," Jesusa said. "Let them take care of you. Soon you can move him. It will be better, my love. Do what Jesusa says…"

"I didn't get the money," Dorie said.

"What is that?"

"I didn't get the money."

"'But what happened?"

"I couldn't. Listen, Jesusa, do you have any money?"

"I have ten thousand *pesos,* more or less," said Jesusa, shocked into simplicity. "It was to start the little business of the dresses from Paris…"

"Will you lend it to me?"

"Ah, little one, and the *Americano* of the forests…?"

"I couldn't…" We are both at the bottom of our resources, she thought. I am about to invent a story, and she is about to be ungenerous. She took Jesusa's hands and laid her wet face in them. "I am sorry, my dear. I should not ask you…"

"Ah, the dresses are not important. It's a crazy idea. You know how one gets these…"

"Let's forget about it for now. We will think of something else," Dorie said.

"No, no, thinking will not do," Jesusa said. "I have decided, I have decided this moment. You shall have the money. You shall have the money, my lovely!"

The priest and Don Emilio left at nightfall. Dorie went back to the room.

"Paco," she said softly. The room was lit only by the corridor lamp. "Are you asleep?"

"No."

"How was your game?"

"Today I lost what I won yesterday."

She sat in the chair beside the bed. "Is it true, what Jesusa says? The priest is dying?" she asked. She felt a sudden, guilty sense of pleasure in being alive.

"I don't know. He is lively. He tells many jokes."

"Does he? How brave. Perhaps he doesn't know yet."

"No different from the rest of us."

"I didn't see Feli's friend," she said. "I didn't get the money. That is, I saw him once, but I could not go back..."

"You didn't..."

"I borrowed it from Jesusa."

He spoke slowly. "From Jesusa? But she is not a well-to-do woman and it will be a difficult thing for her..."

"That is why I asked her."

He was silent. "I thought you must see," she said. She spoke into the darkness, unable to see his face. "The man, you remember, the man in front of the shack, waiting with his rifle, because of something that other man...your relative..."

"Tiburcio Gómez?"

"Yes, because of something he did, long ago. You said that you took on that wrong, when you took on the mine... You said it was..."

"A bond," he said.

"Yes, I wanted...that."

"A bond...with Tiburcio?"

"No, no, with Jesusa!" He doesn't understand, she thought. Why was it so important? But he had been wrapped in his dreams, she thought, while she had been with Jesusa, been a part of this picture here. How could he know? She tried again.

"Yes, with Jesusa. Please listen, please try." She put her face next to his.

"You wanted to stay here. You got your way," he said, as

if trying to recollect something far distant.

"Yes, I had my way." She was blind, instinctual, climbing another dark staircase to have a pain removed.

He encountered her hand in the dark, and laid it on his breast. After a moment he said, "Where would Doña Jesusa have gotten so much money?"

"I don't know. It was to buy some dresses to start a business, some dresses from Paris."

"From Paris. Where would she get some dresses from Paris?"

"In Manzanares, I think she said."

He laughed.

"When you are better," she said, "We will get them for her."

"Yes," he said, "Some Paris dresses, from Manzanares."

The lines were busy at the telephone exchange, then badly ridden with static. She waited on a wooden bench beside a leathery, rum-smelling man who was trying to put a call through to Villavicencio. The operator arranged and rearranged the plugs, summoning the Hotel Lindbergh. Finally Dorie was motioned to a cubicle and Feli's voice came through, very faint.

"Where are you?"

"I am in Pura," she shouted. Everyone shouted into telephones here. "I made other arrangements."

"What about the money? Aren't you going with us?"

"No, no, I have made other arrangements."

"We are very worried…" Some words were lost.

"I am well; I am fine."

"But you are not fine. You're terrible! And he cannot get proper treatment in that terrible place…!" The line began to crackle loudly.

"Listen, Feli," Dorie yelled. "I called because I want you to inform his sister. We haven't written. I want you to tell his sister about the accident. Cautiously. Don't alarm her. Tell her he is recovering."

"What's that? I can't hear…"

"I want you to tell his sister about Paco's being shot. Don't alarm her. Tell her he was injured quite badly and may be lamed…"

"Yes, yes…"

"But say that he will be all right. Tell her that…" she called into the widening distance, "…that he will live. Do you hear me, Feli? Tell her that he will live!"

Acknowledgement

The views expressed of Simón Bolívar in this work are taken from the works of Colombian writer Fernando González.

Books Available from Gival Press
Fiction and Nonfiction

Boy, Lost & Found: Stories by Charles Casillo
    ISBN 13: 978-1-92-8589-33-4, $20.00
    Finalist for the 2007 ForeWord Magazine's Book Award for Gay/Lesbian Fiction
    Runner up for the 2006 DIY Book Festival Award for Compilations/Anthologies
    "…fascinating, often funny…a safari through the perils and joys of gay life."—Edward Field

A Change of Heart by David Garrett Izzo
    ISBN 13: 978-1-928589-18-1, $20.00
    A historical novel about Aldous Huxley and his circle
    "astonishingly alive and accurate."
    —Roger Lathbury, George Mason University

Dead Time / Tiempo muerto by Carlos Rubio
    ISBN 13: 979-1-928589-17-4, $21.00
    Winner of the 2003 Silver Award for Translation, ForeWord Magazine's Book of the Year ~ A bilingual (English/Spanish) novel that captures a tale of love and hate, passion and revenge.

Dreams and Other Ailments / Sueños y otros achaques by Teresa Bevin
    ISBN 13: 978-1-092-8589-13-6, $21.00
    Winner of the 2001 Bronze Award for Translation, ForeWord Magazine's Book of the Year ~ A bilingual (English/Spanish) account of the Latino experience in the USA, filled with humor and hope.

The Gay Herman Melville Reader edited by Ken Schellenberg
    ISBN 13: 978-1-928589-19-8, $16.00
    A superb selection of Melville's homoerotic work, with short commentary.

An Interdisciplinary Introduction to Women's Studies
    edited by Brianne Friel & Robert L. Giron
    ISBN 13: 978-1-928589-29-7, $25.00
    Winner of the 2005 DIY Book Festival Award for Compilations/Anthologies
    A succinct collection of articles for the college student on a variety of topics.

The Last Day of Paradise by Kiki Denis
    ISBN 13: 978-1-928589-32-7, $20.00
    Winner of the 2005 Gival Press Novel Award / Honorary Mention at the 2007 Hollywood Book Festival — This debut novel "…is a slippery in-your-face accelerated rush of sex, hokum, and Greek family life."—Richard Peabody, editor of *Mondo Barbie*

Literatures of the African Diaspora by Yemi D. Ogunyemi
    ISBN 13: 978-1-928589-22-8, $20.00
    An important study of the influences in literatures of the world.

Maximus in Catland by David Garrett Izzo
    ISBN 13: 978-1-92-8589-34-1, $20.00
    "…*Maximus in Catland* has all the necessary ingredients for a successful fairy tale: good and evil, unrequited love and loving loyalty, heroism and ancient wisdom…."
    —Jenny Ivor, author of *Rambles*

Middlebrow Annoyances: American Drama in the 21st Century by Myles Weber
    ISBN 13: 978-1-928589-20-4, $20.00
    Current essays on the American theatre scene.

Secret Memories / Recuerdos secretos by Carlos Rubio
ISBN 13: 978-1-928589-27-3, $21.00
Finalist for the 2005 ForeWord Magazine's Book of the Year Award for Translations
This bilingual (English/Spanish) novel adeptly pulls the reader into the world of the narrator who is vulnerable.

The Smoke Week: Sept. 11-21, 2001 by Ellis Avery
ISBN 13: 978-1-928589-24-2, $15.00
2004 Writer's Notes Magazine Book Award—Notable for Culture / Winner of the Ohionana Library Walter Rumsey Marvin Award
"Here is Witness. Here is Testimony." –Maxine Hong Kingston, author of *The Fifth Book of Peace*

The Spanish Teacher by Barbara de la Cuesta
ISBN 13: 978-1-92858937-2, $20.00
Winner of the 2006 Gival Press Novel Award
"…De la Cuesta's novel maintains an accumulating power which holds onto a reader's attention not only through the forceful figure of Ordóñez, but by demonstrating acutely how ordinary lives are impacted by the underlying social and political landscape. Compelling reading."—Tom Tolnay, publisher, Birch Brook Press and author of *Selling America* and *This is the Forest Primeval*

Tina Springs into Summer / Tina se lanza al verano by Teresa Bevin
ISBN 13: 978-1-928589-28-0, $21.00
2006 Writer's Notes Magazine Book Award—Notable for Young Adult Literature
A bilingual (English/Spanish) compelling story of a youngster from a multi-cultural urban setting and her urgency to fit in.

A Tomb on the Periphery by John Domini
    ISBN 13: 978-1-928589-40-2, $20.00
    This novel a mix of crime, ghost story and portrait of the protagonist continues Domini's tales in contemporary Southern Italy, in the manner of his last novel *Earthquake I.D.*

For a list of poetry published by Gival Press, please visit: *www.givalpress.com*.

Books available via Ingram, the Internet, and other outlets.

Or Write:
    Gival Press, LLC
    PO Box 3812
    Arlington, VA 22203
    703.351.0079

Or Visit: *www.givalpress.com*